IGNITE

A Devil Chaser's MC Romance

L Wilder

PROLOGUE

M Y CHEST FELT tight, and my heartbeat pulsed through my veins. Tears streamed down my mother's face as she tried to explain everything to me. Even though she was obviously upset, I couldn't hear anything she was saying. My eyes drifted over to the baby carrier resting at her feet. My nephew, John Warren, was nestled inside his car seat, and his big green eyes were focused on me. Even with all the commotion going on right beside him, he had such a peaceful expression on his little face. I took a deep breath and tried to pull myself together.

I'd pretty much lost all train of thought as soon as my mom had mentioned my sister. She was trying to explain how Hailey had died from a drug overdose last night, and now she thought John Warren was in danger. I was suddenly overcome with a feeling of panic. How could this happen? My sister. My only sister was dead.

"Lily!" Mom shouted.

My eyes snapped up and locked on hers. "What do you mean Hailey's dead? I just talked to her a couple of days ago, and she was making plans to start rehab! She was getting her life…" I started. I felt like someone had reached inside my chest and grabbed my heart in their fist. I struggled to even take a breath.

"Focus, Lily! We don't have time to go through all of this again! You need to take John Warren and leave before they come looking for him," Mom pleaded.

"You need to give me a minute here.... You just told me that my sister is dead, Mother," I said with more anger than I meant. A million thoughts raced through my head, and I couldn't make sense of any of it. "What are you talking about? Who will come looking for him?"

"I'm sorry, sweetie, but there's no time to explain all of this right now. I've already packed all of his things and put them in your car. You need to pack whatever you can in the next twenty minutes and then, GO!"

"Just wait a damn minute! I need time to think about all this!" I felt totally overwhelmed and confused. Everything was moving too fast, and she wasn't making any sense. "Have you even thought this through? I don't know a damn thing about kids! How am I supposed to take care of an eleven month old baby?"

"Use your instincts. He's a sweet baby, Lily. You'll do fine, and whatever you don't know, you'll figure out."

"Stop! Just...stop! I can't do this! You know this is crazy!" I shouted, feeling my panic rise. My mother had always been my voice of reason, but now she'd gone completely off her rocker.

"Calm down. You don't want to scare him. Lil', you're a smart girl. You *can* do this, and Tessa will be there to help you once you get to Tennessee."

"This is insane, Mom. I can't just leave my life here

and head off to the other side of the country. I have a job… and what about the house? I can't just leave everything behind. Why don't we take John Warren to Maverick? He's his father; he can take care of him."

"You can't be serious, Lily! Haven't you heard anything I've said? Maverick was awful to Hailey! He's the one that got her hooked on all those drugs in the first place. He used her and then threw her out when she was pregnant! And he's *dangerous*. Satan's Fury is even worse than your father's club. They run guns and kill just for the fun of it! They will come looking for John Warren, and we can't let them find him." Mom stood quietly, searching for the right words. I knew she was trying to do the right thing.

After a few seconds, she continued, "I promised Hailey that we'd keep him safe if anything ever happened to her. It's like she knew something was going to happen. She was scared, Lily. I'd take him myself, but they'll come looking for me first. They don't know anything about your cousin Tessa. No one will think of looking for you there," Mom explained.

"Do you think we'll be in danger? Do you really think his club will come looking for us?" I asked. After hearing everything she'd just said, I knew the answer, but I had to ask. I knew if I did this, I would spend the rest of my life looking over my shoulder.

"If you hurry and get out of town, you'll be fine. You just need to play it safe. Don't contact me. I'll get in touch with you as soon as things settle down here," Mom said as she handed me a thick white envelope.

"What's this?" I asked as I looked inside and saw a large amount of money.

"There's enough there to get you started. Find an apartment and a daycare for the baby. I already talked to Tessa, and she said she'd help you get a job as soon as you got there. She's seeing some new guy and promised that they'd take care of you both."

I stood there silently. Even though everything in my life was about to be thrown into a shitstorm, there was no way I could say no. When I looked back over to John Warren, I couldn't help but think of Hailey. His dark hair and that cute lopsided grin remind me so much of her.

I walked over to him and bent down to meet his gaze. He hadn't made a sound since Mom walked into the house with him. I ran my hand over his little head, smoothing the baby fine brown hairs. His mouth curved into a small smile that melted my heart.

"Okay…. Help me pack," I told her.

Once we loaded my car, I buckled John Warren into his car seat and checked my GPS. I quickly realized it would not be an easy trip. It was over thirty-nine hours from Clallam County, Washington to Paris, Tennessee. I'd have to cross seven states to get there, and I wasn't known for my great sense of direction. I'd be lucky if I ever even made it to Tennessee. As I pulled out of that driveway, I instantly knew my life was never going to be the same.

CHAPTER 1

LILY

I FELT RELIEF wash over me when I finally crossed over the Kentucky border. I decided it was time to call Tessa, so I could tell her that we would be there soon. I hadn't seen her in years. The last time I talked to her she had been getting a divorce and was planning to move with the kids to the old lake house.

After a few rings, she answered. "Lily, are you okay?" she asked frantically.

"I'm fine. I'm sorry I haven't called sooner. It's been a long couple of days," I explained.

"I've been worried to death about you. I didn't know what to think when your mother called. She said you were moving here and bringing John Warren with you. What's going on?"

"I wish I knew, Tess. Everything is just so screwed up right now. I feel like I'm running in a hundred different directions, and I haven't even had time to think. Did she tell you about Hailey?" I asked, fighting back the tears.

"She did. I'm so sorry, sweetie. I know that must

have been difficult for you. I remember how close you two used to be. How are you handling everything?" Tessa replied.

"To be honest, I haven't had time to really think about it. John Warren has been a great distraction, but let's just say, he isn't a fan of long car rides. I can't wait to get there."

"Oh! I can only imagine. Bless his little heart. I can't wait to see you both. We found you a great little house not far from Bishop's."

"That sounds perfect. I can't wait to see it." Honestly, I couldn't wait to get John Warren out of that car. I didn't care where, as long as we got there soon.

"Your mom mentioned that you were working as a bartender back in Washington and you were really good at it. Would you be interested in doing that here?"

"I'm not sure how that would work with John Warren. I'd have to find someone to take care of him while I work."

"Let me worry about that. Bishop just lost his bartender at the clubhouse, and I'm sure he'd love to have you work for him. It'll be a little different from what you're used to, but I'll help you figure things out. I hate that you had to spend Thanksgiving on the road. I'll have you plenty of left overs ready when you get here."

"That'd be great. Thanks, Tess. I really appreciate all this. We're going to find a place to stop tonight, and then we'll head that way in the morning. I'll call you when I get closer."

"Great. I can't wait! It's been a long time since I've

had a baby around," she said excitedly.

"Well, get ready. You're about to have your hands full with this little guy. See you tomorrow," I told her as I hung up the phone. After talking to her, I felt a little better about the whole thing.

I couldn't believe how hard the trip had been, and I was more than ready for it to be over. We'd barely made it to Montana when everything went to hell. John Warren had started in with a fit, and he'd let it roll. And I mean ROLL. I never knew a kid could scream like that. It was excruciatingly high-pitched, paint-peeling screaming that would have the best of them running for the hills. I was frantic. I tried everything I could think of to calm him down. I gave him a bottle, changed him again, burped him…. Yeah…I didn't even know if you were supposed to burp an eleven month old. Damn. I didn't have a clue. When I couldn't get him to calm down, I decided to find a place to stay.

The clerk at the hotel gave me a hesitant look when I checked in. John Warren was still having a meltdown, and I'm sure he wasn't excited about giving us a room. I gave him my best look of desperation, and he handed over the key. As soon as we got in the room, I put John Warren in a warm bath, and he immediately stopped his tantrum. He splashed around in the water and smiled. Yeah, the little man likes a bath. That was pretty much the routine for the trip. Drive… meltdown… drive… meltdown.

Now, it was time to find another hotel. We were only a few hours from Paris, but we were both worn out. I found us a cheap hotel in Paducah with a little diner inside. It wasn't as nice as the other hotels where we'd stayed before. The paint was chipping off the walls, and the clerk could barely speak English, but he was sweet and I needed to save our money. Between gas, food, and hotel rooms, it was going fast. We ate a quick dinner and made our way to our room. The room was the same as any random hotel you'd find on the side of a highway, but it was clean, and I didn't feel scared being there alone.

I gave John Warren a bath and put on his pajamas. I laid him next to me and just stared at him. He had to be the prettiest baby I'd ever seen. Those gorgeous green eyes were going to break hearts one day. He had no idea what was going on in the world around him, and it just broke my heart. He didn't know that he'd never see his momma again. He would never hear her sweet voice or feel her soft kisses. He'd never feel her hugs again. Hailey's hugs were the best. You could feel the love radiating from her when she wrapped her arms around you. John Warren was going to miss so many wonderful things. It was just too much.

I felt the warm tears stream down my face as my mind became clouded with thoughts of my sister. Hailey had been going through a hard time, but she'd always loved John Warren. He was all she ever talked about. She always had the funniest stories to share, and I could hear the love in her voice every time she talked about him. She was a good mother, and now she was going to miss everything – not only his first words and steps, but the bigger milestones, like kindergarten and graduation. I continued to cry as I thought of all those lost moments. I truly believed she would've gotten herself together. She'd just needed a little more time.

It didn't matter anymore. She'd never get the chance. Her time had run out and now he was stuck with me. I began to worry, *What if I mess him up?* I knew Mom was concerned about John Warren's safety, but I'd never forgive myself if I screwed up with him. I fell asleep praying that Tessa would be able to help me once we reached Paris.

I had no idea what time I finally nodded off, but I was rudely awakened by a small finger jabbing me in the ear. When I opened my eyes, John Warren had the cutest little smile on his face. It was obvious that he was proud of himself for waking me up.

"Okay, Little Man. I'm up…. I'm up. Time for us to get you changed and ready for another round of torturous driving. I'm sorry, but we gotta do it," I told him as I lifted him off the bed. I changed him and gathered up all of our things. When I checked myself in the mirror, the image was not a pretty one. My eyes were swollen from crying, my hair was a mess, and I already had a stain on my shirt from the leak in John Warren's bottle. Nope, I was not a pretty sight to behold.

I'd just have to suck it up and go. We didn't have much farther left, and I still needed to call Tessa. We would be in Paris in a couple of hours, and I didn't have time to waste on worrying about what I looked like.

CHAPTER 2

GOLIATH

I DON'T KNOW why I thought this Thanksgiving would be any different from all the others. I guess I'm just a glutton for punishment when it comes to my mother. The minute I walked through the front door, I could tell she was wasted. The blinds were drawn, and the TV was muted while she sat in the recliner completely zoned out. I used to get pissed and give her hell hoping that it would make some kind of difference. Now, I'd just stopped trying. I knew that sounded pretty shitty of me, but I'd been trying for years. She wasn't going to change, so I just tried to make the best of it.

"Mom, where's Bryce? Has he been here today?" I asked, knowing that she didn't know the answer.

"Hmmm? I ...," she stammered. "I… uh… think he was here earlier, but had to go take care of something?" she slurred.

My brother was almost as bad as she was, but instead of being addicted to drugs and liquor, he was obsessed with making money. He was some fancy ass lawyer in Memphis, and he didn't like to be associated with the likes of us. He'd called last week promising that he would take the time to check on Mom over the holidays, but he was apparently a no show like always. Prick.

"Have you eaten anything today?" I asked. I hated seeing her like this. She was getting thinner by the day, and her eyes were glossed over. I didn't know how she had survived that long on liquor and cigarettes, but the old gal kept trucking on.

"I ate some cereal earlier," she murmured. "Might have some chicken in the fridge if you want it."

"I thought I'd make us a nice dinner for Thanksgiving," I told her, hoping that she might eat some real food for a change.

"Knock yourself out," she said as she flipped her wrist, dismissing me from the room.

If I didn't still remember the woman she used to be I probably would've walked out the door and never come back. There was a time that I had actually been proud that she was my mother. She had gone to every ball practice, all of our award programs at school, and taken pictures of every crazy thing my brother and I ever did. Everything changed the day my dad was killed. It was late one night when his car swerved into oncoming traffic. He'd hit an eighteen-wheeler head on, and it killed him on impact.

My parents weren't the perfect couple, but I knew they'd loved each other. Mom's face would light up every time he walked through the front door. I remember how he'd pull her in for a kiss when he didn't think we were watching, and he was always holding her hand – in the car... in church... walking into the movies.... He couldn't keep his hands off of her, and just knowing that he loved her like that, made me love him even more.

The day we buried him, my life changed forever. Mom had started drinking and missing work several days a week. It didn't take long for her to get fired, so the drinking just got worse. She stopped fixing dinner and rarely made a trip to the grocery store. Everything just fell apart. My brother left for college, so I was left to take care of Mom. Being a senior in high school, I didn't have a clue how to help her. I tried to hide the bottles and gave her hell any time I saw her drinking. She reeked of alcohol, and I hated seeing her wilt away. I even tried begging her to get help. Nothing seemed to work, so I decided to do what I could to keep her safe and alive, and leave the rest to the good Lord himself. That was over fifteen years ago, and nothing had changed.

I stocked her kitchen with some basic groceries and supplies, and I got everything ready to make the lasagna. It really didn't feel like a Thanksgiving kind of meal, but I figured it was something that might last her a couple of days. I cleaned the kitchen while the lasagna baked in the oven, and ended up taking three bags of garbage to the curb. When the lasagna was done, I was ready to get out of there. She was passed out in the recliner when I walked back into the living room. I leaned over her and gave her a kiss on the cheek. She didn't even budge.

When I made it back to the clubhouse, I noticed most of the guys were still gone. They were all out visiting their families for the long weekend. I grabbed a few beers and headed back to my room. If I was going to be alone tonight, I'd rather be here than back at my house. I turned on the football game and tried not to think about my shitty afternoon. I fell asleep sometime around the third quarter.

Bishop showed up around 11 o'clock the following day. He had that "look" that something was on his mind. He gave me a nod, so I followed him into his office and shut the door.

"Did ya have a good Thanksgiving with Tessa and the kids?" I asked.

"It was good. Ate more than I should've and missed most of the game."

I decided I didn't want to mention how my night sucked, so I changed the subject.

"You seemed to have something on your mind when you walked in. Is everything okay?" I asked.

"Not sure. Tessa's cousin is moving here. She has something going on, but we don't know all the details."

"Anything I can do to help?"

"We'll see. Tessa wants her to run the bar now that Jessica is gone. Not sure how that will work out. I'll have to meet her first and see if I think she'll fit in with all of us."

"Tessa is pretty cool, man. If she thinks this girl can do it, then I'm sure it'll be fine. Does she have any experience?"

"She bartended for a while, but no idea if she's any good at it. She'll have to help out in the kitchen and take up some of the slack around here. This place is a pig sty."

"Yeah, it's gotten out of hand over the past few days. When is she supposed to get here?"

"Later today. Tessa is going to bring her over and show her around. I'd like her to start today if she's up to it. She's been driving for three days, but the guys will be coming in tonight."

"I'm sure it'll be fine. It's not like she'll be mixing a lot of drinks…."

"True. We'll see how it goes."

"I'm going to do a little work in the garage. I'll be around if you need anything," I told him.

"Thanks, man," Bishop replied as his phone began to ring. I left him to his call and headed over to the garage. I wanted to finish up a few things before the guys started rolling in.

Working turned out to be a bad idea. My mood went from bad to worse. I couldn't get the engine in the piece of shit Chevy truck to turn over, and the parts I'd ordered last week still hadn't come in. When I felt the urge to punch the concrete wall, I knew it was time to get the hell out of there.

I walked into the bar and froze. The most devastatingly beautiful redhead I'd ever seen was standing at the bar with a pen hanging from her perfect round mouth. I was immediately jealous of that damn pen.

My body instantly reacted to her. Her delicate features reminded me of an angel. She had amazing green eyes that glowed when the light hit them, and her deep auburn hair barely touched her shoulders. I had to stop myself from reaching out to touch her. There was such an innocence about her. She was like some kind of dream, and I had to see if she was real. At that very moment I became consumed with the overwhelming urge to protect this woman.

She was looking through all of the cabinets and counting the bottles of liquor we had lined against the wall, when she turned toward me and jumped.

"Shit! You scared me half to death! What are you doing just standing there gawking at me like that?" she snapped.

It took me a minute to respond. I wasn't expecting that kind of reaction from her. "I was trying to figure out why a girl like you is standing there behind my bar," I said sarcastically. I remembered Bishop mentioning Tessa's cousin would be working here, but there was no way this could be her.

"What exactly is that supposed to mean? A girl like me?" she said giving me a Go-To-Hell look. "I'm here to bartend, *Einstein*. Why else would I be taking stock of all the liquor?"

"Uh, yeah. That's not gonna happen, little girl. There's no way in hell you're working in this bar," I told her.

"*Excuse* me? What's got your tighty whities in a twist? Bishop hired me to run the bar, and that's exactly what I'm going to do!"

Just as I was about to really lay into her, Taylor opened the front door, and Renegade followed her in carrying a huge box. He had his hands full but still managed to notice the girl the minute he walked in.

His eyes quickly gave her the once over, and he asked, "Who's this?"

Seeing him even look at her pissed me off even more. "This is *nobody*. This is someone who was just about to *leave*," I growled.

She put her hands on her hips and gave an audible huff before she said, "Actually, my name is Lily. I'm the new bartender. I'm taking Jessica's place."

"Nice to meet ya," Renegade replied. He looked over in my direction and smirked as he said, "Looks like it's your turn, Goliath." He laughed out loud as he headed to the garage.

I scowled at him before I turned to Taylor. "This is bullshit. She isn't working here. Hell, she can't be over 18. It would be illegal for her to serve drinks here." I was pissed, and I didn't mind letting them both know it. How could Bishop think she could work there without all the guys putting their damn hands all over her? I loved my brothers, but there was no way I was going to let that happen.

"What's your problem, asshole? I'm 24 years old, and I've been working in a bar bigger than this for over three years. I can definitely handle this place," Lily said defiantly.

"Goliath, just give her a chance. She may be great at this. She doesn't have to do *everything* Jessica did. Just let her bartend and help out around the kitchen for a little while. We'll see how it goes," Taylor said obviously trying to calm me down, but it wasn't working. It was a disaster waiting to happen.

"Yeah. She'll last about a day around here. Do whatever you want, *little girl*. I couldn't care less." I did care, though, and that was the problem. She just seemed too innocent to be working there. The thought of her even being there didn't sit well with me.

"Sure thing, Mr. Personality. Why don't you go pull that corncob out of your ass, and I'll finish getting ready for tonight's party. I'll make it just fine," Lily said as she turned her back to me and began to wipe down the counter at the bar.

My day just kept getting better and better. The hell with what she thought. The clubhouse wasn't the place for a girl like her. Fuck it. I walked out the door and headed for my bike. I needed to get the hell out of there before I did or said something I'd really regret.

CHAPTER 3

LILY

THE BLONDE-HAIRED BEAUTY stood there staring at me with a concerned expression. It was kind of comical that the chick was actually worried about me. She reminded me of my best friend in high school. The kind of girl all the boys pined over but never stood a chance with. Her blonde hair flowed down around her shoulders, and she had an athletic build. It was obvious she took care of herself. Normally, I would have been a little intimidated by someone that attractive, but there was something about her that I already liked.

"You'll just have to ignore him today. There must be something that's bothering him. He's usually not like this," she tried to explain.

"It's me. I'm not sure what I did, but I could tell the minute he saw me, he was put off. I guess I rubbed him the wrong way or something... but he can just get over that shit. I need a job, and I'm not going anywhere," I told her with one of my exaggerated eye rolls.

"My name is Taylor, by the way," the bombshell said as she politely extended her hand.

"Well, nice to meet ya, Taylor. I hope I haven't given you a bad impression. I'm usually not such a bitch," I told her with a warm handshake.

"Don't worry about it. I like a girl who can stand up for herself," she replied with a wink.

"Thanks. Are all the guys like that? Tessa said they were all sweet and would love having me here. But... I'm not off to a very good start."

"The guys are great. Really. You've already met Bishop, he's the club president, and I'm with Renegade, the Sergeant of Arms. Goliath is the VP. You'll meet the rest of the guys tonight. I'm sure they'll love you. Just don't let them give you a hard time. Ha, but from what I've seen, I don't think you'll have a problem with that," she laughed.

"I hope so. I really need this to work out. Tessa has been a lifesaver helping me find a place and lining up this job."

"It'll be great," she smiled. "Look, let's get together later in the week. I'll show you around, and you can tell me all about yourself."

"I'd like that. I'll see you at the party tonight, right?"

"We wouldn't miss it. I better go check on Renegade. If I don't keep an eye on him, he'll be in that garage working and forget all about me being here," she laughed as she headed for the back door. "See ya tonight! Wear something hot. It'll piss Goliath off, but it'll be so much fun to watch!" she added as she shot me a dazzling, devilish smile.

I couldn't help but laugh. I had plenty of sexy little

numbers that I could use to torment him. I'd make him think twice before he called me *little girl* again! I couldn't remember the last time a guy got me riled me up like that.

I mean, you'd have to be blind not to see that the guy was totally hot. Damn. He had to be at least six foot five, and he was built like one of those cage fighters you see on TV. You could see the muscles rippling through his tight black t-shirt every time he moved. His hair barely reached the tips of his shoulders, and he had it brushed back out of his face so you could see his gorgeous eyes. They seemed to change from hazel to dark brown when he became frustrated with me. When he stormed out of the bar, I had to admit, I enjoyed the view. That man had a smoking body. Too bad he had a shitty personality to go with it.

I spent most of the afternoon cleaning and organizing the kitchen in the clubhouse. It was a total mess, but after I finally finished cleaning, it looked pretty awesome. It had a really rustic feel to it. There was a fully stocked kitchen, and a long hallway to bedrooms for the guys. The bar had several tables and an awesome jukebox. There was a long, deep cherry counter with leather barstools facing a huge mirror. It reminded me a lot of my father's clubhouse.

I never got to see my dad very often when I was little. My mother had really hated us having anything to do with him or his *damn* club. She told us that we didn't have any idea how awful he really was, and she'd made a mistake marrying him. She was always reminding us that we should stay away from him and *his kind*. I had a hard time believing everything she said, because I loved him. I never saw him that way, and I wanted to spend time with him. When I was finally old enough to drive, I snuck over to his clubhouse to see him. His clubhouse was awesome, and everyone loved him. He would light up the minute he saw my face, and he was always bragging about me to all of his brothers. I always looked forward to the next time I would get to come see him.

Everything changed the day Big Mike decided he wanted to have a turn with me. I wasn't even sure how I ended up alone in the room with him. He was over-weight, making his gut jet out over his belt. The long hairs on his arms made me cringe when he put his arm around my shoulder. I smelled the booze on his breath, so I knew he'd been drinking. He leaned over and tried to kiss me. I pushed him away, and he didn't know how to take no for an answer. I'd just turned 17, and I wasn't prepared to take on a man like that. He took my throat in his hands and slammed me against the wall. I begged him to let me go. I could barely catch a breath through the tight grip of his fingers. His free hand started to reach between my legs. I could smell the stench of his revolting breath as he told me all the horrible things he wanted to do to me. I started to panic and began kicking and screaming with all my might. It didn't even faze him. Luckily some of the other men came in just as he began undoing my pants. Black spots were swimming in front of my eyes. He dropped me to the ground, grabbed his beer, and acted like nothing had ever happened. I quickly stood up, and without ever looking back, I raced out to my car. I wasn't sure if my dad even knew what had happened with Big Mike. I'd been so freaked out by it, I never went back to his clubhouse. I'd decided Mom must have been right about bikers after all.

I ran back to the house to take a quick shower and finally check in on John Warren. He was down for his nap, and everything seemed to be fine. Tessa arranged for Bishop's neighbor to watch the kids tonight. She assured me that the lady was wonderful, and I didn't have anything to worry about. She hadn't been wrong yet, so I took her word for it. At least I'd be right around the corner if they needed me.

The house Tessa had found for me was perfect. It was really close to the clubhouse, which made it easier for me to check on John Warren when I needed to. It was an older home with two bedrooms, and it was already furnished with the basics. It wasn't anything fancy, but it was a start, and I liked it. Tessa let me borrow Izzie's old crib and helped set it up in the spare bedroom. She'd already bought plenty of groceries for us, so I wouldn't have to worry about that for a while. I would've been lost without her.

Before I went back to the clubhouse, I gave myself one last check in the mirror. I was wearing my best push-up bra with a low cut black t-shirt that showed off my assets and dark skinny jeans with black boots. I put on more makeup than usual to cover up the dark circles under my eyes. I added a little extra dark eyeliner and threw on a few bracelets and a pair of earrings. After running my flat iron through my hair, I was out the door. I didn't have time to give it my all, but I didn't look half bad.

Luckily, I was the first one there. I had time to gather my wits before the guys started showing up. I checked the bar one last time just to be sure I knew where everything was. I didn't want to drop the ball with Bishop there that night. I wanted him to feel good about hiring me.

It didn't take long for everyone to start rolling in. Courtney and Bobby were the first to come up and introduce themselves.

"You must be Lily! Tessa has told me so much about you. I'm Courtney, and this is Bobby," she said, pointing over to the good-looking guy beside her. With a pouty expression, she continued, "The guys around here call him Crack Nut. I'll explain all that later. So, how's it going so far?"

Bobby gave me a chin lift and a smile before he headed over to the pool table. I smiled back, deciding he seemed like a nice enough guy. Hopefully, the rest of the guys would be too.

"Tessa's told me all about you, too. She said you'd be here tonight. Nice to meet ya. And so far... things are going pretty good."

"Well, if you ever need anything, just let me know. I heard all about your nephew. I can't wait to babysit. Tessa has me on the calendar to watch him next week."

"Calendar?" I asked.

"It's a teacher thing. Always planning everything out.

She's made sure that you have a sitter on all the nights that you're working."

"That girl thinks of everything. I don't know what I'd do without her. Can I get you something to drink?"

"Sure! I need a drink or two. It's been a long day," Courtney said, as she plopped down on the stool and rested her arms on the bar.

I grabbed her a beer and asked, "Beer okay? They don't have much to choose from around here. I need to make a liquor run before the next party."

"Yeah, beer is fine. Thanks." She took a drink, and that's the last thing I remember. People started piling into the clubhouse and rushed the bar. Everyone introduced themselves as they asked for their drinks. I barely had time to look up for the first two hours of the party.

When things finally slowed down, I walked to the end of the bar to talk to two of the guys. One of the prospects, a guy named Bulldog, seemed abrasive to me, but the other one, Sheppard, was *very* easy on the eyes. He didn't really have the whole biker look going on. He was clean shaven with short blonde hair, but there was something mysterious about those deep blue eyes. He reminded me of a young Brad Pitt, but Sheppard was rougher around the edges. I always liked that in a man… too bad he was a biker. Off limits.

"You guys need another drink?" I asked.

"Always. Just keep them coming," Bulldog replied. I turned to grab them both a beer out of the cooler, and I could feel their eyes burning a hole in my jeans as I leaned over. I turned back, and Sheppard gave me a lazy grin. Yeah, he was easy on the eyes alright.

"So, Bishop said you moved here recently," Sheppard began with an interested expression. I knew he was hoping to get me to tell my "story", but I didn't want to get into all that yet.

"I always liked it here when I was a kid. It's nice to be back."

"You planning to stay here long?" he asked.

"Not sure. I guess I'll have to see how things go," I said with a nervous laugh. There was no way to be sure. I could only pray that no one found us there.

The front door suddenly flew open, and Goliath sauntered in. Damn. I couldn't take my eyes off of him. My body instantly reacted to him, and I hated myself for it. His eyes met mine, and he continued to stare at me as he walked over to Sheppard and Bulldog.

Sheppard looked over to him and asked, "Where've you been all night? I figured you'd be the first one here." He nodded over in my direction and continued, "Have you met Lily? She's going to be working the bar now."

Goliath raised his eyebrow and gave Sheppard a disgruntled look. "Yeah. I met her," he answered hatefully. "Mind getting me a beer?"

I slowly reached into the cooler and grabbed him a beer from the top. I picked one that wasn't cold and opened it. As I slammed it on the counter, the beer foam immediately began to erupt over the mouth of the bottle. "Here ya go," I said with a devious smile. That'd teach him. What a dick.

He grabbed the bottle off the counter and used his finger to flick the foam off the top. "Thanks for that," he said, giving me an evil glare.

I decided not to respond. I walked to the other end of the bar and offered Courtney and Bobby another beer. Earlier that night they'd seemed to be totally into one another – smiling, kissing, and holding hands. Now, there was a distance between them, and Courtney had a worried expression on her face. I didn't know her well enough to ask her about it yet, but I had a feeling that something was up with the two lovebirds.

CHAPTER 4

GOLIATH

———⊰◦◦◦⊱———

"**W**HAT'S UP WITH that?" Sheppard asked me as he nodded his head over towards Lily.

"Don't get me started, man. Let's just say we didn't hit it off when we met earlier today," I told him.

"She seems like a really nice girl," Otis said, looking in her direction. "She's a friend of Courtney's or something and needs a break. Think she's had a rough go of it."

"What're you talking about?" I asked him.

"I don't know all the details, but she's raising her sister's kid and really needs a job. She doesn't have much help. I think the sister died or something," Sheppard explained.

Well, fuck. I felt like the wind had been knocked out of me. I had no idea that she was going through all that.

"Hell, I'd tap that ass, don't give a shit what her story is," Bulldog said as he peered over at Lily.

"Shut the fuck up, Bull," I snapped. It took all I had not to punch him in the damn face. Asshole.

"I'd watch my step, brother. She's actually Tessa's

cousin, and Bishop's keeping an eye on her. Don't know why she moved here, but I've got a bad feeling about it," Sheppard replied.

"Why's that? You think she's in some kind of trouble?" I asked.

"I'm not saying that for sure, but ya gotta wonder why she moved all the way down here from Washington. That's crazy, man."

He had a point. There had to be more to the story, and I planned to find out exactly what was going on with that girl. She'd been dominating my every thought since the minute I'd laid eyes on her. She'd gotten under my skin, and it was screwing with my head.

While my mind was still focused on Lily, Cindy came up to me and leaned into my shoulder.

"Hey there, sexy. Having a good time tonight?" she asked. She was wearing a tank top that barely covered her breasts and tight leather pants. She was a pretty girl, but she'd never been my type. I'd never showed her any interest, so I didn't know why she kept trying.

"I've had better. How 'bout you?" I asked.

"It'd be better if I was alone somewhere with you," she said as she pressed her breasts against my chest and ran her fingers through the back of my hair. I looked over towards Lily, and she was staring right at us. When our eyes met, she quickly turned away.

"Not tonight, doll. I gotta get to work in the garage early tomorrow," I told her, hoping she'd get the hint.

"Maybe some other time then. I'm planning to bring my friend, Brandie, to the club next week. I've told her all about you, and she can't wait to meet you," she said, running her hand through the ends of my hair.

"She planning on becoming one of the Fallen Girls?"

Cindy nodded her head yes.

"Make sure she knows what she's getting into before you bring her around here."

"Already have. She's all in." She gave me a kiss on my neck and headed over towards Bobby. I just shook my head. We all knew she wasn't gonna get anywhere with him.

I shot a game of pool with Doc and drank a few more beers before I decided to call it a night. I really did have a lot I needed to get done the next day. Before I left for my room, I glanced back over in Lily's direction. Renegade and Taylor had finally made it, and they were talking to Bishop and Tessa. Lily was serving them their drinks and really seemed to be enjoying herself. It actually looked like she was doing a pretty good job of running things. Tessa was talking a mile a minute, and Lily was focused on her conversation when I lifted my beer to Bishop to let him know I was leaving. He lifted his in return and went back to listening to whatever the girls were saying.

When I finally got in the bed, I could still hear the music blaring through the thin walls of my room. I tried turning on the TV for a little distraction, but it couldn't keep my attention. My mind kept wandering to Lily.

There was something about her that I couldn't shake. I couldn't keep myself from worrying about her. The girl had traveled halfway across the country with a kid to boot, and she thought she could handle working in that place. Not to mention the fact that she was the most beautiful thing I'd ever seen. My gut told me I needed to help her, protect her. I just didn't understand why I was so drawn to her. I knew I wasn't going to be able to leave it alone.

I needed to get up early, so I could finish working on that damn Chevy. When I finally got the thing running, I planned to go by and see Lily. It was time that I paid her a visit. I needed her to see that being at the clubhouse, while trying to raise her sister's kid wasn't going to be easy. She needed to understand that working in that bar, with the late hours and drunken idiots, was a recipe for disaster. They might have been my brothers, but I knew they wouldn't hold back when there was a beautiful girl to fight over. I couldn't say that I blamed them. I felt the same way.

CHAPTER 5

LILY

M Y BED HAD to have the worst mattress in the history of the world. I didn't get in until after one in the morning, and I tossed and turned all night. John Warren woke up at the crack of dawn, so I got no sleep whatsoever. I slowly pulled my aching body out of bed and walked down the hall to his new room. I found him in his crib with a bright smile on his face. Just seeing him standing there like that made the long night worth it. I wouldn't trade that moment for anything.

"Hey there, Little Man. I missed you last night," I told him, pulling him up out of the crib. His little baby hands reached for my hair and gave it a tug. "No, John Warren, that hurts!" I shouted while pulling his hands from my hair. He giggled and screeched as I laid him down to change his diaper and clothes.

We headed for the kitchen to get some breakfast and a bottle. I still didn't have a high chair, so I sat him in my lap. That probably wasn't the best idea. I ended up with applesauce handprints all over me. The front of my shirt looked like he'd just played a game of patty cake on my chest. I desperately needed a high chair.

My list of needs was growing by the minute, so I was glad that I'd started working at the clubhouse right away. I was running out of cash and needed to consider finding a second job until I got my feet on the ground.

John Warren sat in front of the small TV in the living room watching Sesame Street and playing with his toys, while I spent over an hour unloading all our stuff. I was pretty impressed with all the things I'd been able to cram into my little car. I'd even managed to shove a few extra blankets and sheets under the seats. I had to say I did a pretty good job packing considering the short amount of time I was given.

After I organized all of my clothes and found a place for the enormous amount of stuff my mother had packed for John Warren, I decided it was time to give the house a good cleaning. I found a bottle of bleach and went to town cleaning every corner of that little house. The overwhelming fumes made me dizzy, so I decided it was time for a break. I was just about to go into the kitchen to make myself a cup of coffee when the sound of a loud motorcycle engine caught my attention. It sounded like it pulled into my driveway. A few seconds later, someone was pounding on my door.

I almost lost my mind when I looked out the window and saw Goliath standing there. Of course, he looked amazing in his black Guns and Roses t-shirt and jeans. His hair wasn't brushed back, and I liked the way it fell across his face. I looked down at my stained shirt and bleached shorts and knew I looked like a damn mess. I knew the dark circles under my eyes had only gotten worse throughout the day and my hair was matted down with sweat and filth. Shit. Why the hell was he there anyway? I pulled the door open and surprise washed over his face.

He cleared his throat before he said, "Damn. You look like shit."

"Well, aren't you a ray of sunshine this morning?" I huffed. I stood there a moment just staring at him before I said, "Why don't you go spread the wonder of your *charming* personality with someone else today? I'm not in the mood." I turned away from him and tried to shut the door in his face.

His foot blocked me from closing the door as he pushed his way through. Without saying a word, he sauntered into the living room. His head moved back and forth as he checked out everything in the room. I even saw him inspecting the locks on my windows! Then, he made his way towards the kitchen. He spent a few seconds there before he started down the hall towards the bedrooms.

"Wait! What the hell do you think you're doing?" I asked, following him into John Warren's room. He never even responded to me. He just walked around the house like he owned the place, checking everything out.

"Look, you really need to leave. I have a lot to do, and I don't have time for this right now… or *ever* for that matter!" My voice was slowly rising to a scream, but he didn't even flinch. He just waltzed back into the living room and knelt down over John Warren.

An innocent smile spread across his face as he turned to me and asked, "What's his name?"

"John Warren. It's almost time for his bottle and nap, so umm… yeah," I told him, hoping he would get the hint and just leave.

"I'll give it to him while you take a shower," he said as he picked John Warren up and cradled him in his arms. Oh shit, that wasn't good. A sexy as hell biker holding a baby would make any girl weak in the knees, and bikers were totally off my *to do* list. No. Not going there. There was too much history with bikers in my family, and I wasn't about to let it repeat itself with me.

"No, I've got this. I'm sure you have things to do. So, go forth and prosper," I said, motioning him out the door.

"Go get me the damn bottle and take a shower. Trust me. You need it," he demanded as his eyes roamed over my body.

"Screw you, Goliath. Where do you get off coming in here telling me what to do?" I shouted.

"Get the bottle, Lily!" he demanded.

To hell with it. I threw my hands up in the air and stormed into the kitchen for the bottle. The nerve of him! I made a show of slamming each and every cabinet door shut. I did the same thing with every drawer in that damn kitchen. It didn't help calm my anger. When I made it back into the living room, Goliath was already sitting in the old recliner with John Warren waiting for me. He gave me a sexy grin as I shoved the bottle in his hand and headed for the bathroom.

I hated to admit it, but a hot shower was exactly what I needed. It was amazing. The warm water eased my aching muscles and as an added bonus I no longer smelled like bleach. I took my time washing my hair and even shaved my legs, since I knew John Warren was okay. I was dreading going back into the living room to face Goliath, so I took a little longer than I normally would've drying my hair and getting dressed.

When I finally made my way back, John Warren had fallen asleep in Goliath's arms. I wanted to stand there and just stare at them both. Seeing such a strong man be so gentle was more than my mind could take. I needed to get him out of my house, before I did something I would regret. I walked over to him and lifted the baby out of his arms. I took John Warren to his room and laid him down in his crib.

Goliath was waiting for me when I returned. He stood by the door looking devilishly handsome, and my body immediately reacted to him. I hated that I found him so irresistible, but I couldn't help myself. There was something about him that kept drawing me in. Even though my mind was telling me no, my body had other plans. I had walked over to him without even realizing it. I was standing in front of him, his eyes locked on mine. He brushed the loose strands of my hair behind my ear, and I felt the need to reach out and touch him. Before I had a chance to think, he brought his hands to the sides of my face, gently pulling me closer to him. His lips pressed against mine, and my knees instantly felt weak. I should've pushed him away. I should've told him to get the hell out, but I was lost in his touch. His tongue brushed against my mouth encouraging me to open, and I couldn't find it in myself to deny him. I felt my pulse quicken as the kiss became heated. His hand began to roam over my body. I knew I should stop him, but I couldn't pull away. His hands reached up for my breasts, caressing them firmly. There was more pleasure than pain. It surprised me how much I liked it. He was igniting a fire in me that I knew I'd never be able to put out. He released me from our embrace, and I hated the sense of loss my body felt. Damn.

He took a step back, his eyes slowly roaming over me with a concerned look. I didn't know why he stopped the kiss, but from the look on his face, I knew I wouldn't like it.

He brought his hand up to my chin, forcing me to look at him and said, "You need to get some sleep." Where the hell did that come from? One minute he was kissing me, and the next he was back to treating me like a child.

"I'm *fine*. You can stop treating me like a child, Goliath."

"Just get some rest, Lily." He kissed my forehead and turned towards the door. I watched in stunned silence as he walked out, heading for his bike. The roar of his engine starting pulled me from my trance.

So many thoughts swam through my head. I hated to admit it, but he was probably right. I really did need to get some rest. The late nights were going to be tough. If I was going to keep my job, I'd have to find a way to make it all work.

CHAPTER 6

GOLIATH

I HAD TONS of work to do today, but I promised Renegade that I would head up to Kentucky with him. Taylor's lease was up on her old apartment, and I agreed to help him get the rest of her things.

We took Bishop's truck and spent the two-hour drive talking about the club. Renegade was making big plans for Christmas. Apparently, he was planning to ask Taylor to marry him. She'd meant everything to him for years, but it'd taken some trouble with another club to make him admit that he couldn't live without her.

"I can't believe you're finally doing it, man. I'm glad you finally realized all the other bullshit just didn't matter," I told him.

"She deserves better, man, but I'm done letting that stand in my way. She's stuck with me now."

"Glad to hear it."

"What about you?" Renegade asked.

"What about *me*? You know I don't have anyone I'm interested in," I argued, trying not to remember the touch of Lily's lips or the taste of her. I failed.

"That's bullshit. It was pretty obvious that morning in the bar that Lily was getting to you. You better make your move," Renegade said, laughing out.

"She's a pain in the ass, man, and she won't listen to a damn thing I say," I explained. That was the understatement of the year.

Renegade gave me a thoughtful look and said, "It's been a long time since I've seen anyone get to you like that. She's definitely made an impression."

"Yeah, well… I made an impression on her, too. She pretty much hates me, and that's probably the best thing for both of us."

"Don't do that, man. Learn from my mistakes and stop trying to convince yourself that it couldn't work. I wasted a lot of time doing that with Taylor."

Renegade didn't say anything after that. He let his words linger in the air for a while. I knew he was right. There was definitely something about Lily that was fucking with my head. Even though she was the most infuriating woman I'd ever met, I had an overwhelming need to be near her. Hell, I wanted to go back to her right then. I needed to find out what it was about her that was driving me so crazy.

It took us over two hours to load all of Taylor's stuff into Bishop's truck. It wouldn't have taken us that long if Renegade hadn't spent an hour next door talking to her old neighbor. He just *had* to go check in on her. She sent us home with a batch of cookies and some kind of chicken casserole. It made the truck smell like a mix of chocolate and chicken. I wasn't a fan of chocolate and chicken. It was going to be a long drive back.

When we got back in town, Renegade dropped me off at the clubhouse. I told him I would come by the next day to help him unload everything. It had been a long day, and I was ready to grab a beer and go to bed.

The bar was pretty quiet when I walked in. A couple of the guys were playing a game of pool, and Lily was talking to Sheppard over at the bar. She had her elbows propped on the bar and a finger twirling her hair as she talked. Immediately a rush of heat curled in my gut and radiated throughout my body. I clenched my fists, and my jaw tightened as I watched them together. I froze when Sheppard's hand grazed her as he pushed her hair back over her shoulder. My blood was boiling. I knew I was jealous. I hated the thought of anyone's hands on Lily but mine. I walked over to the bar, and neither one of them noticed me. Hell that pissed me off even more.

"I'd love to go with you sometime. It's been a long time since I've been on a motorcycle. I used to love to ride with my dad when I was younger, but it's been awhile," Lily told Sheppard with a fucking sexy as hell smile. Damn it.

"I'll take you one day next week. We can make a stop by Hidden Creek on the way back and grab dinner," Sheppard replied. He was smiling at her like he had just won the damn lottery. *Motherfucker!*

"That's not gonna happen," I said before I even had time to think. They both turned and looked at me with surprise.

Lily straightened her back and raised her eyebrow.

Her face flushed with anger, and she seemed to be thinking of what to say when Sheppard cleared his throat.

He turned to me and questioned, "And why's that?"

"Don't," Lily said to Sheppard, raising her hand up to stop him. She turned her fury towards me and said, "What the hell is your problem?"

"No problem, Lily. Everything is just *fine*. I'm just clearing things up for my friend here," I said, feeling my anger rise.

"What exactly are you *clearing up*, Goliath? Do tell. I'm very interested to hear this." She crossed her arms over her chest drawing my eyes to her perfect tits. I still remembered the feel of them pressed against me, and I had to fight to keep my composure.

I stepped closer to her and replied, "I'm letting Sheppard know that the only bike that you, *little girl*, will ever ride… will… be… *mine*."

A stunned expression crossed her face as the red in her cheeks darkened. She threw her arms in the air and shouted, "Well, it's official. You are completely, totally, without a doubt… *delusional!*"

"Was I delusional when your tongue was down my throat?"

Sheppard stood and gave me a silent nod as he headed over to the pool table. He knew that this conversation was over where we were concerned.

"Sheppard! Wait. Don't let him…" Lily called out to him.

"It's fine, Lily. I'll catch up with you later," Sheppard

called back as he waved over his shoulder.

"I can't believe you just did that!" Lily whispered angrily with her brows furrowed and her lips pursed.

I slipped my hand behind the nape of her neck and pulled her closer. I could feel her pulse race against the tips of my fingers as I leaned in towards her and whispered in her ear, "I was only stating the facts, Lil'. When you get ready for that ride, you just let me know." I released her from my grasp and gave her a wink, before I reached over the bar and pulled a beer from the cooler. She was obviously flustered, and I liked it. She was even more beautiful when she was pissed. Smirking, I turned and walked back to my room, locking the door. I tugged off my shirt and pants before I stretched out on my bed and turned out the lights.

My mind wouldn't shut off. I kept imagining her leaning over that bar. Those amazing tits almost spilling out of her low-cut top. Now that I knew exactly how those damn things felt? Hell, I was on fire for her. Visions of her haunted my thoughts as I took my hard dick in my hand. I closed my eyes as I imagined her straddling me while I sat on the edge of one of the bar stools. Her bare skin pressed against me as she began riding me *hard* – her breasts close to my face as I watched her grind against me. I moved my hand up and down my throbbing cock. I imagined how tight she would feel coming all over me. I could feel my release approaching. I pictured her screaming out my name… her body falling limp from exertion. The image pushed me over the edge and I exploded in my own hand, but it didn't satisfy me. She would be mine.

CHAPTER 7

LILY

W HAT THE hell? I had no idea what'd just happened, but I did *not* like how my body became
consumed with need when Goliath touched me. I could
still feel the warmth of his breath against my neck, and I
had to fight the urge to touch where his hand had held
me. Crap. I'd been going crazy since we'd kissed. I
couldn't seem to get myself under control. I wanted
him… but I couldn't let it happen. I looked over in
Sheppard's direction, and he was still playing pool with
Doc. He never did come back over to the bar, but I
noticed that he kept staring at me when he didn't think I
was looking. I wasn't sure who I was more frustrated
with – Goliath or him. I decided to give up trying to
figure it out. It was late, and I needed to pick up John
Warren from Tessa's.

When I pulled up in their driveway, all the lights
were off except for the kitchen. I walked around back
and tapped on the door. Bishop opened the door
wearing a white t-shirt and lounge pants. John Warren
was propped up on his hip holding his bottle in his little

hands. Tessa was a lucky girl. Even with his tired eyes and messy hair, the man was hot. He gave me a smile and gestured for me to come in.

"Hey, I'm sorry it's so late. Has he kept you up?" I asked.

"He just had a hard time getting settled tonight. It was fine. Tessa seems to think he has a hard time being away from you," he explained.

"I feel the same way. It's hard being away from him, but I'm doing the best I can under the circumstances. I'll have to figure something out sooner or later, though. I can't keep getting him up in the middle of the night like this." I reached to take him from Bishop, and as soon as he was in my arms, he rested his head on my shoulder. Poor baby was wiped out.

"I had an idea that might make things a little easier for you both. It would take a little work, but I think it'll help," Bishop told me.

"I'm up for anything at this point. What are you thinking?"

"We have an empty room at the clubhouse. One of the brothers was killed a while back, and no one has been using his room. I thought we might set up a place for the little man there."

"I don't know, Bishop. I can't leave him alone while I'm working."

"Tessa will help you work all that out. It wouldn't be all the time. We can try it on slow nights when there won't be many people around. Doc's wife, Melinda, and Cindy can also help out when he's there."

It sounded like a great idea. I really liked the thought of having him closer to me. "Okay. It'll take me a few days to get things set up, but I'd like to try it. Thank you, Bishop. You and Tessa have done so much for me. I don't know how I'll ever repay you."

"Stop thanking me, Lily. You're doing a great job at the clubhouse. Hell, that place was a mess until you showed up. We should be thanking you. Now, go home and get some sleep," he said. He opened the door and waited as I loaded John Warren into the car. He waited until I was out of the driveway before he headed inside and turned out the lights.

John Warren was sound asleep before I ever made it home. I carefully pulled him out of his car seat and carried him inside. I knew I should go put him in his crib, but I wanted to spend some time with him. I sat in the recliner and laid him across my chest with his head on my shoulder. I rubbed my hand softly over his back and gently kissed the top of his head. I could feel his chest slowly rise and fall and the warmth of his breath against my neck. I closed my eyes and just listened to his soft breathing.

It was such a wonderful feeling to have him close to me like that. It helped center me and make everything seem less significant. I was stressing over nothing. Goliath and I couldn't happen. Besides, it wasn't as if a man like him would ever see me as a girl they wanted to get involved with. I had too much baggage. No man wanted that in their life. No. I needed to focus on taking care of John Warren and stop daydreaming. I was just being stupid.

I didn't even realize I had fallen asleep until the sun started to shine through the cheap window blinds. I carefully lifted John Warren up and carried him into his room to lay him down in his crib. It was still early, so I hoped he would sleep just a little bit longer. I went to my room and laid down in my bed, pulling the covers over my head. I needed at least another hour of sleep. I was still exhausted.

Three hours later, I heard John Warren babbling from his crib. I rolled over, took a deep breath, and struggled to get out of bed. I definitely needed to find a new mattress soon or that thing was going to kill me. As I walked down the hall, I could hear the springs of his bed bouncing up and down. I slowly walked into the room and found him jumping at the end of the crib while holding tightly to the back rails.

"Good morning, sweetheart. You look happy this morning," I told him as I reached over and picked him up. "We have a lot to do today, Little Man. We've gotta get dressed and head to town to do some shopping." I twirled him in the air, and he giggled and squealed. I loved hearing him laugh. It made the whole place seem brighter.

After another messy breakfast, we headed into town. I had a long list of things to buy but not much money left. After we went to the grocery store, I decided to look in a used furniture store for a crib and a high chair. I was a little surprised to see how much they cost, so I decided that I'd have to wait on the high chair. I needed the crib for the clubhouse more. I paid the lady and told her I would come back for the crib as soon as I could borrow someone's truck.

When we got back home, the dirty dishes in the sink seemed to be taunting me. I hated washing dishes more than anything in the world. I really needed a dishwasher, but there was no way I could afford that anytime soon. I turned on the hot water and started filling up the sink. When it was about halfway full, water started spraying out all over the kitchen. Something had broken loose from the faucet, and water was shooting straight up in the air. I quickly reached under the sink and turned the water off. I was soaked. Damn. I hated to call Tessa, but I had to get it fixed. She'd know a plumber that I could call.

CHAPTER 8

GOLIATH

T ODAY WAS A busy day in the garage. Everyone was busy working on different projects that had to get finished. I enjoyed spending time at the garage with my brothers. It didn't even feel like work. We were doing what we loved, and we were able to do it together. It didn't get any better than that.

We had several remodels to complete before the end of the week, and Bishop asked me to make a run for him. He wanted me to go to Texas to pick up two cars that needed a complete overhaul before Christmas. I'd have to leave later in the week, and I would be gone for several days.

"You can take Bulldog with you. It'll be a quick turnaround. You should be back here by Sunday afternoon," Bishop explained.

"No problem. Just get the details worked out, and I'll take care of it," I told him. He was about to say something when his phone rang. He reached into his back pocket and pulled out his phone. He smiled when he looked to see who was calling.

"Hey, baby. You missing me already?" he asked with amusement in his voice.

He listened for a moment, then said, "Yeah, I think he's a good plumber, but tell her I can fix it. Just be sure to tell Lily to keep the water off until I get there."

He waited a second and then said, "Love you, too. I'll be home in a few hours. I'll grab dinner on the way home. Tell Drake I'm bringing Chinese, and I'll be sure to get extra egg rolls." He laughed as he hung up the phone.

"What's going on at Lily's?" I asked.

"Tessa said something is wrong with her sink, and she needed a plumber. I need to run over there and see if I can fix it. Pretty big mess from the sound of it," he explained.

"I'll take care of it," I told him.

"You sure?" Bishop asked. He gave me one of his looks, but he didn't push.

"I got it. I had a couple of other things I planned to do over there anyways."

"Okay. Give me a shout if you need a hand," Bishop said as I headed for the garage. I needed to grab my tools before I left.

When I got to her house, there was a plumber service van sitting in her driveway. It looked like she had already handled her issue with her water, but I decided I'd make sure she wasn't getting ripped off.

Lily was more than a little surprised when she opened the door and found me standing on her front step. I could see the plumber standing behind her, and it looked like he was writing her a quote.

"What are you doing here?" she asked, crossing her arms across her chest.

"I'm here to fix the sink."

"I've already taken care of that, Goliath," she replied as she looked over to the plumber. He finished whatever he was writing and brought it over to her. She took the paper out of his hand, and her eyes grew wide when she saw the price.

"Three hundred and eighty dollars for a faucet? You have got to be kidding me," she said with an angry tone.

"That covers the parts and labor, Miss," the asshole told her.

I wanted to wring his neck for trying to take advantage of her, but before I could say anything, she said, "Thank you for coming by today. I'll have to wait a few weeks before I can afford that. I'll call you."

"Whatever you say," the guy told her as he walked past me out to his van.

She looked over to me and said, "Don't even start, Goliath. I have this handled," she said firmly.

"You *handled* it? Waiting a few weeks to fix your sink isn't handling it, Lily."

"Well, that's the best I can do."

"Let me fix the damn sink. It'll just take a few minutes, and then you won't have to go without it. There's no point in waiting when I can do it now."

She stood there mulling over what she should do. I considered pushing harder, but she nodded her head and moved to the side so I could walk in.

"Good girl." I followed her into the kitchen, tossed my tools onto the floor, and started taking out the old faucet. She stood there staring at me for a minute before she let out an exasperated sigh and left the room. Once I began removing it, I realized the ball valve had gone out, so the entire faucet would need to be replaced.

Lily was in the living room with John Warren when I walked into the room. "I've gotta run into town. Gonna need to get a new faucet."

She looked up and said, "Umm... bring back the receipt, so I can pay you back when I get paid." I could tell from her expression that she didn't want me to know that she didn't have enough money right then.

"I'll take care of it. I'll be back in a few minutes. Just leave everything alone until I get back," I told her as I bent down and placed a small kiss on her cheek. I left before she had a chance to argue. I didn't want to get into a fight over it. I just wanted to get what I needed so I could fix the damn sink.

It didn't take me long to get everything I needed from one of the local appliance stores. Lily was waiting for me in the kitchen when I walked back into the house. I dropped the bag on the counter and started taking everything out of it.

"How much was it?" she asked with a seriously aggravated tone.

"Don't make a big deal out of this."

"I'm going to pay you back, Goliath. I just need to know how much I owe you."

"I'll tell you what... if you'll *just leave* and let me do

this in peace, we'll call it even."

She sighed loudly and shook her head as she walked out of the kitchen. I watched her go, not able to tear my eyes away from her perfect ass. With a groan, I decided to try and get her ass out of my mind and get some work done. It took several minutes to loosen all the rusted screws, some of them were completely stripped. As soon as I removed them, I lifted the old faucet, and water spilled out of the old valve, soaking my shirt. Damn. I pulled off my t-shirt and shoved part of it into my back pocket. I crawled back under the sink and began installing the new faucet. I heard Lily walk back into the kitchen, but she stopped at the edge of the door.

I bent my neck so I could see what she was doing. Her eyes were slowly making their way up my legs and froze when they reached my bare chest. She was totally focused on my tattoos. I cleared my throat, and her eyes finally moved up to meet mine. Her cheeks flushed with embarrassment.

"Need something?" I asked.

"Mmm…umm. No, I was just… seeing if you needed any help," she stammered.

"I've got it. I'll be done in a minute, and then I'll fix those broken locks on your living room windows."

"Windows? You don't need to fix my windows. They're just fine!"

"You need to be able to lock all of your windows, Lily. It isn't safe." She stood there with a puzzled look until the sounds of John Warren's cry snapped her attention away from me. She quickly turned and raced down the hallway towards his room.

I finished up the faucet and headed into the living room where Lily sat on the floor with John Warren.

"Are you hungry, sweet boy?" she asked, lifting him up into her arms. I watched as she carried him into the kitchen and got out his lunch. She had everything laid out on the table. She sat him in her lap and began feeding him.

"Where's his high chair?" I asked.

"We're making do with what we have right now. I'll get one soon," she said.

"Well, that explains the mess on your shirt the other day," I told her as I laughed.

"That's not funny, you big jerk," she said as she flipped me off. "Sometimes he's just not very nice, John Warren," she told him laughing.

"The kid needs a nickname."

"I'm sure you'll think of something," she said while throwing a towel at me. "Why don't you dry off before you catch a cold?"

She smiled as I wrapped the towel around my neck and headed for the living room. By the time I finished fixing the two broken locks, she'd finished feeding John Warren. I was putting my damp shirt back on when she walked in. A smirk crossed her face as she watched me pull it over my chest, and I could tell she liked what she saw.

"You're all set," I told her feeling proud that she was a little bit safer in the old house.

"Thanks, Goliath. I really do appreciate it," she said

softly as she tucked a few loose strands of hair behind her ear.

"Ahh… little girl has a sweet side to her after all. I like that."

CHAPTER 9

LILY

I COULDN'T SEEM to make my mind up about the guy. My heart almost beat out of my chest when I walked into that kitchen and saw him sprawled out under the sink. I couldn't stop my eyes from wandering all over his body. I thought my panties were going to burn off my body when I saw the tattoos on his bare chest. I wanted to reach out and run my fingers over the different colors of ink that marked him. He was beautiful, and it was messing with my head. It didn't help matters that he was being so nice fixing things around the house. I really did appreciate everything he did, but then he'd open his mouth and everything would go straight to hell. I thought if he called me *little girl* one more time, I might punch him in the throat.

"You know… we'd get along a lot better if you just never opened your mouth," I told him.

He looked intensely at me and said, "One day soon, I'll change your mind about that." He stepped a little closer, towering over me. He gently tucked a few loose strands of hair behind my ear, and when goosebumps pebbled across my skin, the corners of his mouth curled into a sexy smile. He brushed the back of his hand across my cheek and said, "I have to head back to the club. Is there anything else you need?"

My eyes were locked on his, and I couldn't move. He was standing so close that I found it difficult to speak. My knees felt weak, and I could feel my heart racing beneath my chest. I cleared my throat and said, "Nope. All good here." He gave me one of his sexy winks and turned towards the door to leave.

Shortly after, I heard him pull out of the driveway. I stood there looking around the house, and it just seemed empty without his presence. I really didn't want to be in the house alone, so I decided to take John Warren to the park. It was pretty warm outside, and I figured he would enjoy the fresh air.

We spent several hours playing at the park, and by the time we got back, I was exhausted. That kid loved to swing. I'd have to find a way to get one for the backyard soon. I loved watching him smile and laugh. It made me a little homesick being there alone with him. I wish I could call and check on Mom. Not being able to talk to her made me feel like I'd lost my sister *and* my mother. I just needed to know if she was okay. I knew I needed to wait for her to contact me, but it was getting harder every day. I didn't know how much longer I could hold out.

After dinner, I gave John Warren a bath and put on his pajamas. The long week had finally caught up with me, and I wanted to get to bed early. I didn't really want to be alone. I decided to give him his bottle in my room so I could have him close to me. I turned on the TV, lowering the volume, and laid him in the bed next to me. As soon as he finished his bottle, he fell fast asleep. I lay there staring at him, wondering if it was possible to ever love him any more than I did right then. It amazed me how quickly he had completely stolen my heart. I couldn't imagine ever being without him. I pulled him closer to me and finally fell asleep.

The next morning, I was brought out of my sleeping stupor by the faint sounds of tapping outside my front door. I threw the covers back and went to see what was making that irritating noise. When I peeked out the front door, all I could see were two large boots standing on the steps to a ladder that led up to my roof. I couldn't see who it was, so I had to walk outside to get a good look. When I looked up, I saw Goliath putting up a new security light just above my front door.

"Do you have any idea what time it is?" I asked, placing my hands on my hips.

He never even glanced down in my direction. He was focused on screwing in the light when he said, "Sorry. I know it's early, but I wanted to get this done before I headed to the garage."

"Do you really think all that is necessary?" I asked waving my hand towards the light he was installing.

"Yeah, I do," he said. He finally looked down at me, and his eyes suddenly widened with surprise. The screwdriver fumbled in his hands, and he almost dropped it as his eyes were drawn to my breasts. I looked down and quickly realized that I didn't have on a bra. My thin white t-shirt didn't leave much to the imagination, and to make matters worse, it was cold outside. He was getting an eye full. Damn. I looked back up at him, and he had a huge fucking grin on his face. I could feel the heat rush over my face and felt the urge to cover myself. I didn't want to give him the satisfaction of knowing that I was embarrassed, so I just flipped him off. I could hear him laughing as I stomped back into the house, slamming the door behind me.

I decided to just stay in the house until he was finished. I took a long shower while John Warren was still sleeping and even had time to fix my hair before he got up. I was finishing my makeup when he finally let me know he was ready to eat. I was actually feeling human when I sat him down for breakfast. I felt good and ready to face the day, when there was a loud knock on the door.

I propped John Warren on my hip and opened the door only to find Goliath leaning against the doorframe.

He smiled and said, "Good morning, JW. I hope I didn't wake you up this morning," he said with a sweet smile.

I guess he'd thought of John Warren's new nickname. I liked it. He ran the tip of his finger down the baby's nose. John Warren reached out his little arms and leaned forward towards Goliath. Without any signs of protest, Goliath took him from my arms. They both looked over to me with a big smile.

"You could run a train through here, and he could

sleep through it," I told him. Before I could stop myself, I asked, "You want a cup of coffee before you go?"

"Yeah, I'd like that," he answered, following me back into the kitchen. I poured him a cup of coffee and pointed over to the cream and sugar. Then, I grabbed a couple of jars of baby food and sat them on the table. I retrieved John Warren from Goliath and sat him on my lap so I could feed him.

"You seriously need a high chair, babe," he said with a concerned look.

"You seriously don't know when to give it a rest, do you?" I told him as I began feeding John Warren. "And I *will* be paying you back for the faucet and that new light."

"Have you always been this stubborn, or is it just with me?" he asked.

"I'm being practical, not stubborn. I have to set priorities right now. I don't have a lot of money to throw around at the moment," I explained.

"I get it, but just so you know, you aren't paying me back. We had the extra lights at the clubhouse, so stop worrying about it," he said as he took a drink of his coffee. He kept staring at John Warren. He seemed lost in his thoughts, and I wondered what he was thinking.

"You want some more coffee?" I asked, breaking him from his silence.

"Thanks, but I've gotta get going," he said, standing up to leave.

"Okay. Will I see you tomorrow night?" I asked.

He stared at me with a strange look on his face that I

couldn't really read, but I wanted to.

"Do you want to?" he asked.

I wanted to deny it, but I couldn't. Staring into his eyes, I found myself answering honestly.

"I think I do."

He leaned down and brushed his lips against mine. I wanted more, and my tongue danced along his lips, but John Warren picked right then to laugh, breaking the moment.

His hand came up and brushed along the side of my neck. Without thinking, I leaned into his hand, loving the warmth of his touch. He placed another kiss on my forehead before stepping back.

"Then, I'll definitely be around," he said, walking out of the kitchen. "Try to stay out of trouble," he called back before he shut the front door.

When the door closed, I felt a sadness come over me. I didn't want him to go. Damn. I really shouldn't have liked him, but I did. Against my better judgment, I was falling for a biker. My heart was telling me that there was more to him than I had realized. Something that I was deathly afraid that I couldn't live without.

CHAPTER 10

GOLIATH

B ISHOP CALLED ME early that morning and said we needed to all meet. We usually covered all club business on Tuesday night during church, but he said he had information we needed to hear. I was concerned. Bishop didn't call us together like that unless it was important.

When he walked into the clubhouse, he had an intense look on his face. I wish I'd had time to talk to him before the meeting so I knew what the fuck was going on. He stood in front of us, collecting his thoughts before he finally spoke.

"There's a new club moving into town. Snake called me last night to give me a heads up." Snake was the president of the Red Dragons. We'd had a run-in with his club a while back, when one of their brothers attacked Taylor. Things had worked out in our favor, and we'd even ended up helping Snake out. Apparently, he felt the need to return the favor.

"We gonna have a problem with them?" I asked.

"They're called the Black Diamonds. Young group of

delinquents causing trouble wherever they go. They have no code. Constantly adding new members just so they can build up their numbers."

"Who's in charge?" I asked.

"No idea. That's all Snake had to share," Bishop replied, glaring at Renegade. "Look, we don't want these guys causing problems, so keep your eyes open. Let me know if you see anything I need to know about." He turned to Bobby and said,

"Crack Nut, you need to do your thing. See if anyone's bought any property in the area that might be a clubhouse. Anything you find, share it with Goliath and Renegade."

"You got it, Pres." Bobby replied.

"We've got a big order coming in. We need to do our best to make sure everything's done on time. The club's name is at stake here. If this order goes well, it could lead to some pretty big offers in the future," Bishop told us.

"We're on it," Sheppard told him.

"It's also time we consider adding to the club. We need new blood. We've lost men, and those losses can never be replaced, but we gotta fill this table. Do any of you know anyone who might be looking to prospect?"

"Yeah, I've got someone in mind. My cousin, Levi, might be interested. He's coming home from Afghanistan in a couple of weeks. I'll talk to him about it. I figure his friend, Conner, will want to join with him," Sheppard said.

Bishop nodded his head and said, "Good. That's all. Meeting adjourned."

I followed Bishop into his office. I wanted to know if there was more that I needed to know.

"What kind of trouble do you think this club is gonna bring?" I asked.

"Snake mentioned drug trafficking, but said these guys don't mess around. We need to be ready for whatever they bring."

"Keep me posted. If you need me, call. I'm heading over to Lily's."

Bishop nodded, and I headed out the door. I didn't want to be late. I hadn't mentioned anything about the whole babysitting thing to Lily. I figured she'd just try to talk me out of it. I'd asked Tessa to add me to her "calendar" after meeting JW for the first time. I really liked the little guy and wanted to get to know him better. I knew he came as a package deal with Lily, so he and I needed to get better acquainted.

I took a few things with me just in case Little Man needed some distraction. It'd been awhile since I'd been around a kid his size, so I needed to be prepared. I knocked on her door, steeling myself for a fight I knew was coming. The door crept open, and Lily stood there wearing only a tiny bathrobe that barely covered the top of her thighs. I couldn't stop the smile that spread across my face as she tried to tug and pull the robe farther down over her legs.

She finally gave up trying to cover herself and smiled, "What are you doing here? Sorry, but I don't have anything for you to fix today."

"I doubt that, but I'm not here for that. Actually here

to babysit JW tonight," I told her as I moved my body in front of the box I'd brought. I was trying to block her view of the new high chair I just bought.

"Babysit? Seriously?" she asked.

"Yep. Tessa added me to the calendar. Now, go finish getting ready. I have this under control."

"Seriously?" she asked again.

"Seriously. Now, go get your cute ass in there and finish getting ready."

"Why are you babysitting? I thought…."

"Babe, as much as I'm enjoying the view, if you don't go get a move on, you're gonna be late. Tessa called, I'm here. Now, go get ready."

She looked down, remembering what she was wearing and to my surprise, left. I watched her walk away, feeling my dick jump as the cheeks of her ass peeped out with every step she took. Hell. I pulled my eyes from her, but it wasn't easy. I was almost disappointed she'd given up so easily. I liked arguing with her. She got a fire in her eyes when she was mad, and damn, I was quickly getting addicted to the way they sparked and came alive. I was sure I'd piss her off again soon enough, though. I was looking forward to it.

JW was playing on the floor when I walked over to him. I dropped the high chair box in the corner and started pulling out a few of the toys I'd bought. I handed him the small football first. Every kid needed to know the ins and outs of football. He took it in his tiny hands and squealed. Score. Guess he liked it. I'd bought a small basketball goal, but I was going to have to put it together before he could play with it. I'd started pulling out the different parts and the directions when Lily walked in. Damn, she looked good. She was wearing a grey sweater dress with black leggings and boots. Her silver bracelets hung low on her wrists, and I let my eyes travel over her body slowly, enjoying the view.

"Goliath? Don't you think you might have gone a little overboard here?" she asked, shaking her head with her hands on her hips.

I just shrugged my shoulders. I doubted I needed all that stuff, but it was better to be safe than sorry.

"Well…" she gestured to all the boxes and toys lying on the ground, "this is a little extreme."

"What can I say?" I said, trying to sound innocent. "I'm a man that likes to be prepared," I told her with a smile, wondering how it was going to play out.

She rolled her eyes and laughed, but just before she turned to head for the door, a new expression crossed her face. She was obviously pissed as she noticed the new high chair I'd stashed in the corner. "You didn't!"

"The kid needs a damn high chair, Lily."

"I can't believe you did that! …And I was getting him one when I could afford it, Goliath! I told you that!" she yelled. "I don't have time for this, but I promise you, this conversation is NOT over!" she turned and walked out the door, slamming it behind her.

I knew it would piss her off when I bought the damn thing, but she needed it, so I got it. I wanted to help her. It made me feel good to buy her something she needed. So why the hell did I feel like shit about it?

"You know your Aunt Lily wants to kill me right now," I said, looking over at JW. He smiled, shoving the end of the football in his mouth. "Dude, you're supposed to throw it, not eat it!" He never even acknowledged me and kept on chewing.

After I put the high chair together, I brought it into the kitchen to feed JW. As soon as he got in the seat, he smiled and started slapping his hands on the tray. I could tell that he liked it. I just hoped that Lily would like it, too, once she got over being pissed about it. I fed him a couple of jars of baby food, and I was impressed that he didn't make a huge mess. Plus one for me. I gave him a quick bath and put on his pajamas.

"Let's grab your bottle and see what's on SportsCenter tonight," I told him, carrying him into the living room. I found the station I was looking for on the TV and cradled him in my arms with his bottle. It looked like he was about to fall asleep, but he just couldn't get settled. He tried to wrestle out of my arms, and when that didn't work, he started to cry.

Cry isn't really the right word for what he did. A tantrum. A meltdown. Hell, the kid totally freaked out. I decided to see if he needed to be changed. That didn't help. I thought he didn't like the pajamas I put on him, so I changed his clothes. That didn't help. I was running out of ideas, so I decided he needed a distraction. I knew it was cold outside, but I figured it was worth a shot. I propped him on my hip and walked out to the front porch. The cold air must have done the trick, because the crying finally stopped. His little hands grabbed onto my shirt as he looked up at me. I'm sure he was wondering what I was doing.

"Dude, that was a pretty good fit you were having in there. You all done?"

He seemed to be over whatever was bothering him, so I took him back inside. I got us settled in the chair and gave him the rest of his bottle. It didn't take long before he fell sound asleep. I figured it wouldn't hurt to hold him until my show was over.

I WAS A little surprised when Lily lifted JW from my arms and headed down the hall. I must have dozed off. I didn't hear her come in. I stood up and stretched, waiting for her to come back.

When she walked back into the living room, she looked tired. I knew the late hours were tough on her, but she never complained. "How'd it go tonight?" I asked.

"It was pretty slow. Not many of the guys showed up. They really don't need me during the week. Not even sure why I was there," she explained.

"Things will pick up when it gets warmer. Most of the guys stay home when it's cold like this. Enjoy it while you can," I told her.

"Was John Warren okay for you?" she asked.

"Yeah, he's a great kid."

"Good, thanks for sitting with him. I really appreciate it," she said yawning.

I hated to leave, but I knew she needed to get some sleep. I stepped closer to her and said, "I'm going to head out. Get some sleep, and I'll see you later in the week." I kissed her lightly on her cheek, and I headed for the door.

"Goliath?"

I turned back and asked, "Yeah?"

"Thanks," she said softly. I liked sweet Lily. I liked all the different sides to her, but sweet Lily was my favorite.

"Good night, Lily," I told her before I walked out the door. It was a good night. I really enjoyed being there with JW. He was small, but he had personality. He wasn't afraid to let you know when he wasn't happy about something, but even then, he wasn't that hard to deal with. It didn't take much to make him happy, and there was just something kind of cool about having a baby fall asleep in your arms. I could do that every day of the week. Yeah, that kid made me realize that I wanted something more out of my life.

It'd only been two days since I last saw Lily, but it felt like much longer. I'd been busy with work and hadn't been able to see her, but that didn't mean she hadn't been on my mind. She was all I'd been able to think about. She was supposed to be at the clubhouse any minute for her shift, and I couldn't keep my eyes off the front door.

When the door opened, I reacted before thinking. She stopped mid-step when she saw me charging towards her. Her eyes were wide with surprise as she saw the angry expression on my face. I didn't stop until I was face to face with her. I took a moment to let my eyes travel over her outfit one last time before I spoke. She was wearing a mini-skirt with tall black boots and a dark red sweater. The short skirt barely covered the top of her thighs, and the low-cut V-neck sweater was cut way too fucking low. She took a step back when I let out a deep growl of frustration.

"Go home and change, Lil'. You aren't wearing that here," I told her firmly.

She looked down at her outfit and then looked back up to me with an angry expression. "What's wrong with what I'm wearing? It's a skirt with boots, Goliath. I like this outfit!" she scowled.

"I didn't say I didn't like it. I said to go home and change."

"I'm not changing, Goliath. There is absolutely nothing wrong with what I'm wearing," she said, raising her eyebrow defiantly.

"You can do this the easy way or the hard way, but you *are* changing. Period." I could feel the vein in my neck pulsing as my anger continued to rise. She was changing out of that damn outfit even if I had to change her myself.

"Go to hell," she said, trying to push past me so she could get to the bar. I ducked my shoulder into her stomach and wrapped my arms around the back of her legs, lifting her up. Once I wrestled her over my shoulder, she began pounding her fists into my back.

"Put me down, asshole!" she shouted.

"I gave you a chance to do things the easy way. Now, we'll do things my way," I told her, carrying her out of the bar. She continued to hit and scream all the way to my truck. When she started to kick her legs, I reached up and slapped her on the ass. Hard. Her body went still with shock. I was a little surprised that I didn't get more of a reaction out of her, but I was glad she stopped fighting me. I opened the passenger door and tossed her inside. I slammed the door shut and headed over to the driver's side. She sat defiantly with her arms crossed and just stared at me with fire in her eyes.

"You are *insane*. You know that, right?" she said furiously.

I didn't even respond. I was too angry with her. As soon as we pulled into her driveway, she opened her door and stormed into the house. I followed her inside and waited for her to change. She was making a point to take her time, and I was losing my patience. I started down the hall to tell her to hurry up, when I heard her talking to herself. I couldn't make out what she was saying so I continued to get closer to her room. When I reached her doorway, I noticed that she hadn't shut the door all the way. Her angry voice drew my attention to the back corner of her room. She was standing with her back to me, and she was only wearing a pair of black lace panties. I couldn't have looked away even if I'd tried. Seeing her like that made me lose all sense of decency.

She kept mumbling to herself, as she pulled a long sleeve t-shirt over her bare breasts. She was perfect. I closed my eyes and imagined her pressed against me – the scent of her skin, the warmth of her touch. I was consumed with need. I wanted her so badly that it actually hurt not to touch her. I was completely lost in thought, when her door flew open. She was wearing only the t-shirt and panties and was clearly shocked to see me standing there.

"What are you doing?!" she screeched.

"I… I was… Hurry up. I was coming down here to tell you to hurry up. How long does it take to throw on a damn pair of jeans, Lily?"

CHAPTER 11

LILY

WHAT THE HELL was wrong with me? I wasn't the kind of girl that let a man tell me what to do. I made my own decisions. Yet, there I was, in my room, changing clothes because he didn't like what I was wearing. It was insane. I wasn't going to do it! He wasn't going to push me around like that. Hell no.

I grabbed my t-shirt and pulled it over my head, trying to think about how I was going to deal with him. He had to know that he couldn't keep treating me like some child. I opened my door and found him standing there. I had no idea how long he'd been standing there, but he looked lost in his own thoughts.

"What are you doing?"

"I… I was… Hurry up. I was coming down here to tell you to hurry up. How long does it take to throw on a damn pair of jeans, Lily?" he said with frustration.

"I really don't get you, Goliath. What makes you think…?" I let out a deep sigh. I took a moment and looked into his eyes, searching for the answers that I needed from him. His words were harsh, but the look in his eyes told so much more than what he said.

"Why are you doing this?" I said softly. I wanted him to open up to me, to explain why he was acting that way. "Why was it so important to you that I come back here and change?"

"You really don't know?" he asked, leaning in closer to me. He gently brushed my hair behind my ear, never losing eye contact. His eyes both threatened me and adored me at the same time. They burned me down to my soul.

"Tell me. Please, Goliath. I need to know," I pleaded.

He paused, searching for his words. He took a step closer, and I could feel the warmth of his breath on my neck as he whispered in my ear, "A light radiates from you, Lily, and I want to do everything I can to protect it. Even if that means pissing you off by making you cover up that hot little body of yours. Do you even know what it would do to me if one of those assholes put their hands on you? I wouldn't be able to hold back."

"I can handle it, Goliath. I'm stronger than you think," I told him.

"You're one of the strongest people I know. You're a fighter. When someone tells you that you can't do something, there's a fire inside of you fighting to prove them wrong," he said shaking his head. A small smile crossed his face as he continued, "The way your nose crinkles when you're mad. That's about the cutest thing I've ever seen. But then there's Sweet Lily…. The few times I've seen Sweet Lily are my favorite. I'd do just about anything for that side of you."

"Goliath...." I didn't even know what to say. He'd given me more than I ever expected by sharing that with me.

"I don't want to take chances on anything happening to you. You think you have to do all this on your own, but you don't have to. You just have to trust me."

I stood there staring at him, unable to put my feelings into words. There were too many things I wanted to say, but none of them seemed important anymore.

"I know I'm getting to you, and you're fighting it.... Hell, we've both been fighting it, but I'll tell you now... *I'm not letting you go*," he said as he brought his hands up to my face and pressed his lips to mine. His arms wrapped around my waist, and I could feel my body ignite with his touch. The kiss was gentle, but when I pressed my body against his and opened my mouth to him, he couldn't hold back. The kiss was demanding and intense. He kissed me with all the urgency and need we'd both felt over the past few weeks. It was like nothing I had ever felt before. I couldn't get enough of him. I moaned as his hands roamed over my back and rested on my ass, pulling me closer to him. I reached up, my fingers tangling in his hair, urging him on, demanding more. He lifted my legs up around his waist as he slammed my back against the wall. I tilted my hips, grinding against his erection. I wanted more of him. Needed him.

A deep growl vibrated through his chest as he released me from our embrace. He slowly lowered my feet to the floor, and I immediately felt the loss of our connection. He brought his hand to my chin, tilted my head, and forced me to look at him.

"More than I ever imagined."

"What?" I asked.

"Eager Lily. She's more than I ever imagined." I could see the lust in his eyes, and I knew he wanted more, but he didn't take it. Instead, he kissed me lightly on my forehead and said, "I need to get you back. They'll wonder where you are."

"Okay," I replied as I took the tips of my fingers and ran them over my lips. I liked the way they felt swollen from our kiss. He did that. He made me *want* to be marked by him.

Without saying another word, I went back to my room, shutting the door behind me. When I walked back to the living room wearing my jeans and boots, all I got was a nod of approval from him. It was enough. I understood why it was important to him. I didn't necessarily agree with him, but I understood. That was all I needed for right then.

When we finally made it back to the clubhouse, several of the guys were gathered around the bar talking with Cindy and some hot little number I'd never seen before. She was standing between Otis and Sheppard, and she seemed to have their full attention. She had curly dark brown, almost black, hair that was draped over her shoulder. She was wearing dark skinny jeans with tall black boots and a black leather jacket. She was trying to look like a biker babe, but something just didn't fit. With her heavy makeup and large breasts, she looked like she should've had her legs wrapped around a pole, not a bike.

When I walked up, Sheppard gave me a bright smile and said, "There she is. Now, you can all stop your bitching."

"Sorry, I'm late guys. I had to run home for a minute," I tried to explain. They all smiled and gave me nods hello, easing my worry about being late.

"I want a beer, doll," the slut bag said, flipping her hair to the side.

"Okay. Anyone else need anything?" I asked as I made my way behind the bar. There was something about her that just grated on my nerves, but I didn't want to seem like a bitch about it.

"Grab us all a beer," Otis said, ogling his new fantasy girl. Otis was the youngest member in the club, and he still had a lot to learn. He was covered in tattoos and piercings, but he still had that schoolboy look. His skin was tan, but still showed signs of acne. He was slim but muscular. It was obvious that he tried to take care of himself. The new hot momma slipped her arm around his. She stepped closer to him, shoving her tits in his face as she reached for her beer. Yeah. She was really getting on my nerves.

Cindy walked over to me and motioned to the new chick, "This is Brandie. You'll be seeing lots of her, since she's decided to be one of the new Fallen girls."

Brandie watched to see my reaction, but I didn't give anything away. I knew I shouldn't care what those girls did at the clubhouse, but it bothered me. I didn't like why they were there, and I didn't want to have any part of it.

"Nice to meet you, Brandie. If you need anything, just let me know," I told her with the fakest smile I could muster.

Brandie's eyes left mine when she noticed Goliath walking in our direction. Her eyes seductively roamed over him as he approached the bar. I could hear a faint sigh escape her lungs as she took him in. When he reached for the beer I had placed on the bar for him, Brandie made her move. She slipped out of Otis's grasp and walked straight up to Goliath. She pressed the palms of hands against his chest and let them slowly wander down towards his hips. Yep, I was pretty sure I was gonna have to hurt her.

"Aren't you a tall drink of water?" she said, letting her eyes roam over his body. "I'd like to climb you like a tree, handsome. Why don't we go somewhere and get to know each other a little better?" she purred. What a slut bag! I bet having sex with her was like throwing a hot dog down a hallway.

I knew I wouldn't be able to hide my jealousy, so I turned my back to them, making myself busy throwing away all the empty beer bottles. I couldn't make out what they were saying because of the loud crashes the bottles made when they hit the metal trash can. When I turned back around, Goliath had her hand and was leading her down the hall. My heart dropped. It felt like someone had ripped it out of my chest and thrown it on the floor.

My throat tightened, and I instantly felt like I was going to be sick as the bile rose from my stomach.

How could I be so stupid? I knew that was the kind of life bikers led, but I was dumb enough to think things were different with Goliath. I was such a fucking idiot. My imagination was running wild. I wondered if he was kissing her, just like he'd kissed me less than thirty minutes ago. Did she have her legs wrapped around him, wanting him to take her right there at the club? Of course she did. That's why she was there. Fuck! He told me to trust him, and he took that trust and stomped it in the ground. I felt like such a damn fool.

I was about to really lose it. I wanted to take those empty bottles and slam them against the wall. I was just about to do something reckless when Brandie came walking back into the bar. She was smiling, but I saw her brush away a tear from under her eyelashes. The corners of her eye makeup were smudged, and I could tell that she'd been crying. What the hell was that about? I looked back towards the hall and saw Goliath standing there with his arms crossed, staring at me. Relief washed over me when I realized nothing had happened between them, but the look on his face worried me. I had no doubt that my worry had been written all over my face, and now he was pissed. He knew I didn't trust him, and I didn't know what to say to him. The truth was, I really didn't know him well enough to know what he'd do with a girl like that. He'd never given me any reason not to trust him, but I couldn't stop myself from thinking the worst. My heart was still aching, but now it was for a different reason. It hurt because I knew I had hurt him.

My eyes locked with his. I stood there waiting to see what he would say, waiting for him to say 'I told you so', or to say *something*…. Instead, I got nothing. He shook his head and walked past me, heading over to the pool table. He grabbed a pool stick and began playing a game with Doc and Melinda. He never looked back over in my direction. I'd screwed up, and I knew it.

Brandie seemed totally unaffected by whatever had transpired between them. She was back flirting with Otis and Sheppard, and they were loving it. I rolled my eyes and decided to just try and keep busy. I was relieved when Courtney walked through the front door. She was alone, but she gave me a big smile when she noticed me at the bar.

She rushed over to me like she was about to burst and said, "Guess what!"

"What!" I said trying to sound excited.

"Bobby said he wanted to take me somewhere special over my Christmas break! I think he has something planned. Do you think he's going to give me a jacket like Taylor's?"

"I'd say he's a complete idiot if he doesn't. It's obvious that he's crazy over you, girl. Maybe he's finally coming to his senses."

"I hope so. I really do love him," she explained.

"You don't have to tell me. Anyone can see that. You two are perfect for each other," I told her. When she laughed, I couldn't help but laugh with her. I really liked her, and I was glad she was so excited. I hoped he wouldn't screw it up.

"Tessa and Taylor are on their way. We need to plan a girl's night out. Maybe next weekend we could head over to Matt's and go dancing!"

"I'd like that. I'll have to see if I can find someone to run the bar for me," I told her.

"Doc could do it. He was filling in for Jessica before you got hired. I'll get Tessa to set it up. Yay! I love girl's night! Do you like to dance? I love to dance! I haven't been in such a long time. Bobby doesn't like to dance very much, so I haven't gotten to go. This is gonna be sooo great!" she said excitedly.

I looked in Goliath's direction, and he was still avoiding me. At first, it pissed me off that he was acting that way. It was a legitimate mistake. He was being a complete asshole, but I couldn't stop looking over at him. I missed the warmth of his eyes on me. Oddly enough, it made me feel safe knowing he was watching over me. Now, I felt a little lost. Like part of myself was missing.

"You got something on your mind? You seem like you're in a different world over there," Courtney asked.

"I'm fine. It's just been a long day."

"I know what you mean. This time of year is always tough. The kids at school have completely checked out. They could care less about Mesopotamia and Sargon. They are all about getting out of school, so they can stay up all night talking to their friends. I feel like I'm wasting my time even being there."

Tessa walked up just as Courtney was explaining how

bad things were at school, and said, "Amen to that! They're driving me out of my mind. If one more kid throws an eraser across the room, I'm going to string them up by their toes like a piñata!" We all laughed. I had no idea how they did it. There was no way I could be stuck in a classroom full of kids all day long.

"Have y'all met the new girl yet?" I asked, nodding my head over in Brandie's direction.

"Bishop told me about her, but I haven't met her yet. What do you think of her?" Tessa asked.

"You'll see for yourself. Just sit back and enjoy the show. She's good... real good," I said sarcastically. Tessa raised her eyebrow and looked over at Brandie. She was nestled between Sheppard's legs. She had her arms wrapped around his neck while her fingers played with his hair. He was eating it up. Her breasts were pressed against his chest, and he was absolutely loving every minute of it. Yes, he was definitely getting laid that night.

"Oh my god! Isn't Cindy enough? Now, we have to deal with that hoochie momma. I'm gonna end up losing it on one of these girls before it's all said and done. They get on my last damn nerve," Courtney huffed.

"Just ignore them, Court. The new will wear off of this chick before the night is over, and the guys will find something else to obsess over," Tessa said, trying to smooth things over.

Courtney let out a deep sigh and said, "You're right. I'm sure she's a lovely girl." She rolled her eyes, and we all laughed out hysterically. Several of the guys looked over in our direction, and I laughed even harder.

I had a great time with Courtney and Tessa. I loved hearing all their funny stories from school. It sounded like they had their hands full, but I knew they adored the kids they were working with. It was getting late, so everyone had started to leave. Tessa and Courtney both gave me a hug before they left. Courtney looked back over her shoulder and smiled as Bobby took her hand leading her out of the bar.

I was gathering up all the empty beer bottles from the bar when Goliath walked over to Bulldog. Bull had been drinking pretty heavily with Doc and looked more than a little drunk.

Goliath gave him a harsh look and said, "Time to call it a night. We need to leave early tomorrow. We have a long drive, and I don't want to be stuck in the truck with you while you're nursing a hangover."

"I know. I'm finishing up this last beer, and then I'm heading out," Bulldog replied. Goliath never even glanced in my direction. He turned and headed for the door. He was still punishing me for earlier, and I was over it. He was being a jerk, and I intended to call him out on it. I followed him outside. The bar door slammed behind me as I tried to catch him before he reached his bike.

He was several feet in front of me when I called out, "Goliath?"

He slowed down, but he didn't stop walking. "Goliath, will you stop already?"

"I need to get going, Lily. I have a long few days ahead of me, and I need to get some sleep," he said flatly.

He turned and faced me with a flash of rage in his eyes. I knew I had done the wrong thing, but he was being ridiculous. He took a few steps and stopped when he was close enough for me to feel the heat coming from his body. He let out a deep sigh before he spoke.

"Tell me, Lily. What did you think was going to happen with me and that girl tonight?" he asked in a deep, angry voice.

"What was I supposed to think, Goliath? She was gorgeous, and she was practically begging you to fuck her right there in the bar. The next thing I know you're leading her down the hall towards your bedroom," I explained. I thought I'd made several valid points. How could he not see that it looked bad?

"Just so we're clear, I took her into the hallway to let her know without any doubt that nothing would *ever* happen between us. There's only one girl that I want." He took a deep breath and looked to the ground before he said, "The problem is the girl I want thinks I'm the kind of man that just likes to get my dick wet with any random chick. That doesn't sit well with me, Lily."

"Again, how was I supposed to know that, Goliath?" I asked.

"After the kiss tonight, I thought I made myself clear, but I'll tell you what, when you get this whole thing figured out, just let me know." He lifted his leg over his bike and started the engine. Before he pulled out of the parking lot, he said, "I don't share, Lily, and I wouldn't expect you to either."

I watched his tail lights fade away as he pulled out onto the main road. I let his words soak in, and I knew I had screwed up. I hated that he was leaving, but maybe the distance would do us both some good.

CHAPTER 12

GOLIATH

I HAD FIGURED Bulldog would have one hell of a hangover the next morning, but he surprised me by being early. He had the truck packed and was ready to go by the time I got the directions and invoices from Bishop. He'd more than proved himself over the past few weeks, and I needed to talk to Bishop about patching him in. We'd made him wait long enough. Besides, Sheppard had mentioned earlier that he was ready for us to meet the new potential prospects, so we'd have some new guys to do all the grunt work. It was time to make Bulldog a brother.

"We're all set, man. You want me to drive?" Bulldog asked.

"I'll drive the first few hours. You can take over when we stop for lunch," I told him.

"Sounds good. You need anything else before we go?" he asked. He was really pulling out all the stops, and I liked that about him.

"I'm good, Bull. Let's get going. It's going to be a long day. I'd like to get to Dallas before dark. We can stop there and still make it to Austin before lunch tomorrow." I wasn't a big fan of long drives, but I'd always wanted to go to Texas.

We stopped in Memphis to grab some lunch at one of the local barbeque joints. Bull ordered enough ribs for three people, but he ate every last bite, leaving nothing but the bones. I hadn't had much sleep, so I decided to let him drive awhile. I needed to take a break. As soon as I closed my eyes, I found myself thinking about Lily. I could almost smell the scent of her perfume as I thought about her legs wrapped around my waist. She was eager and wasn't afraid to show it. I'd wanted to take her right there in that hallway, but I knew it was too soon. I needed her to know that she could trust me.

I learned the hard way that she hadn't figured that out yet. It pissed me off that she thought I'd have anything to do with Brandie after the kiss we shared. I still didn't understand why she would ever doubt that she was all that I wanted, all that I needed. She was every-thing I'd been waiting for and more. In time she would figure it out, or I'd have to be more persuasive.

The road to Austin was a long one. The endless rice fields in Arkansas made me feel relieved to see the Texas border. Hot Springs seemed like a place I'd like to go back to, but nothing else really drew my attention. Bulldog was sound asleep with his head pressed against the passenger side window. He'd tried to act like the night before hadn't gotten to him, but I knew he'd had too much to drink. I would let him drive more when he felt up to it.

We found a cheap motel just outside of Austin that had a little diner attached to it. After we checked in, we walked over to the tiny diner for dinner. The place was clean but looked dated. It could've used a little TLC, but I didn't care as long as the food was good. I was starving. I wasn't a big fan of barbeque like Bulldog. I just wanted a big cheeseburger and a beer followed by a hot shower.

"I heard that Sheppard is bringing a few new guys in next week," Bulldog said as he took a pull from his beer.

"That's what he said." I knew he wanted more, but I planned to make him work for it.

"Yeah... that's cool. I mean, the more the merrier, right?"

"Yep," I replied, trying to hold back my smile. I figured he had to know that we planned to patch him in soon, but I could tell he was having his doubts.

"Sheppard's a cool guy. I'm sure if he thinks these new prospects are a good fit for the club, then they'll do just fine. Word is they served in the military, so at least they'll know what it means to have each other's back." He looked down at his bottle, and damn if I didn't start to feel a little sorry for the guy. It just wasn't fun anymore.

"Bull, your time is coming soon. Very soon. Just be patient," I told him, hoping that he would know what I was implying. A big smile spread across his face as he gave me a nod. Yeah, he knew what I meant.

"I want to get going early in the morning. Would like to be back home late tomorrow night or early Sunday morning," I told him.

"You got it, man. I figure we're gonna have a few busy weeks ahead of us if we plan to get all these orders done by Christmas."

"There's no doubt about that. Bishop will be on our asses if we don't them done on time. It shouldn't be a problem with the new guys coming in next week. We'll put them to work and get this stuff knocked out early."

"Yeah, it'll be nice having a few extra sets of hands," Bulldog said smiling. He knew he wouldn't be stuck doing all the grunt work. Hell, I couldn't blame him. We'd been using him for all kinds of shit over the past eight months. The guy deserved a little retribution.

We finished our dinner and headed over to the hotel. It was nothing to write home about. The place was a dump. The mattresses were lumpy, and there was no flat screen TV, just an old box model from the 80's. At least the picture was good, so we were able to watch a little SportsCenter before bed. I had a mild obsession with sports – all sports. My dad used to always call me into the living room to see some wild play someone had made, and it became our thing. Every time I saw a great catch or tackle, I thought of him.

Bulldog fell asleep as soon as his head hit the pillow, but I was wide awake. My mind kept drifting back to Lily. I wondered what she was doing right then. Was she in bed curled under the covers wearing a t-shirt and her sexy lace panties? I didn't need to let my mind go there. Bull may have been asleep, but he was still just one bed over from me. I closed my eyes and tried to think about the garage or the game we'd just watched or Christmas with my mother. Nothing worked. I finally fell asleep thinking about Lily wearing that thin white t-shirt and no bra. I loved the expression on her face when she saw me gawking at her. The girl had spunk, and I liked it. Almost as much as I liked the way her tits looked in that shirt. She was perfect.

The drive back wasn't as bad as I thought it would be. We pulled into Paris around 1:30 in the morning. When we dropped off the trailer at the garage, the clubhouse was empty. Apparently it wasn't a big night at the bar. I was standing by the main gate thanking Bulldog, when I noticed two motorcycles driving by. They were creeping by, obviously trying to get a look at the clubhouse. I pulled my keys out of my pocket and headed for my bike. By the time I made it out to the main road, they were already gone. Crack Nut Bobby would need to check our surveillance videos. I didn't want to take any chances.

I was beat. It'd been a long night, so I headed to my room. As much as I wanted to sleep in my own bed, I was too exhausted to drive any further. I wanted to get some sleep so I could get up and head over to see Lily. I was done being pissed at her. At first, it had really bothered me that she didn't trust me, but I'd realized it just meant I needed to prove myself to her. I didn't have a problem with working for it. She was worth it.

CHAPTER 13

LILY

————◦⊙◦————

I 'D HAD THE weekend from hell. I wish I'd never even gotten out of the bed. I didn't sleep at all. I kept thinking of the way things were left with Goliath. I felt torn. Part of me thought he was a big fat jerk for not seeing my side of the situation, and the other part of me felt like crap that I thought the worst of him. We were both right. That's all there was to it. He just needed to give me a break and understand that I needed time to figure everything out. Then again... that's just what he'd done.

To make matters worse, JW was teething. He had been crying non-stop since he got up that morning, and I just didn't know what else to do for him. Tessa told me to give him some children's pain reliever and some teething toys, but he was still cranky. I didn't expect it to be such a big deal since he already had several teeth, but it'd been awful. Fortunately, Tessa said it would be better in a few days.

Since he wasn't feeling well, I decided it was time to get the spare room ready for him at the clubhouse.

Sheppard helped me get the crib from the used furniture store and even help me set it up. He was a little distant, but I didn't care. I was just happy to get some help. After we got everything set up, I spent the afternoon cleaning the kitchen and taking inventory at the bar. I needed to go shopping, so I decided to go see Bishop.

"Bishop?" I asked tapping on his office door.

"Yeah, Lily, come on in. You need something?" he asked.

"We're running low on supplies and beer. I need to make a run to town," I told him.

"Here, take my card. Get anything you need," he said reaching into his wallet for his credit card.

"Thanks. Is there anything I can get you while I'm out?" I asked.

"Yeah, can you see if you can find some more of that cheddar Chex-mix? I love that stuff, but Tessa never remembers to buy it," he said hopefully.

"I'll find it. Be back in a few hours. I'll have John Warren with me, so it might take me a while."

"Don't do that. Bring him to me. I like hanging out with him. I'll give him the grand tour of the place," he said smiling.

"Are you sure?"

"Absolutely."

"Okay. I'll hurry. Thanks, Bishop," I said on my way out the door.

"I already told you about that!" he called back. I smiled knowing that I would never be able to stop thanking him. He was just too good to me.

It took longer than I planned to get everything we needed from town. I didn't realize how much I had to buy. I got several odd looks as I filled my car with all the groceries and alcohol. I was already exhausted by the time I unloaded everything, and the night hadn't even started yet.

At least things were slow at the bar. Apparently the guys had all decided to hang out at Hidden Creek, so the night seemed to drag on forever. I was really starting to miss Goliath. I found myself watching the front door hoping that he would come back early. I just wanted to see his face, to know that everything was okay, but he never came. For reasons I didn't understand, my heart ached for him. My feelings for him had snuck up on me, and now there was nothing I could do about it. I was falling for the big brute, and I wanted him home.

Things never did pick up at the bar, so Bishop sent me home early. He also paid me with a little bonus for all the work I'd done in the kitchen. I was thrilled to have my first check. I had been getting really low on funds, and it was starting to make me nervous. Now, I had more than enough to take care of everything.

Saturday was more of the same. I spent the day cooking several casseroles for the guys, washed my car, took John Warren to the park, and got ready for work. I decided to try taking John Warren with me to work. The room was ready, and I figured it was time to try it out. Melinda said she would love to help me with him, so everything was taken care of.

The night was long. The guys were not in good

moods, and they were all set on fixing it with booze. They were not pleasant to say the least. I did my best to just serve them their beers and stay out of their way. Brandie and Cindy were doing their best to cheer them up, but none of them seemed the least bit interested in either of them. That made me smile.

The guys' bad moods were starting to rub off on me. I was getting a little down in the swamps, and I was really homesick. I really wanted to talk to my sister about everything that was going on with Goliath. I'd even talk to my mother about it at that point, but I couldn't call her. It was just too risky. By then, I was even missing my dad. The more I was around the guys at the club, the more I realized that my mother might have been wrong about him. I knew in my heart that he loved me, and I wanted so much to talk to him again. I was starting to think it was time for me to try to contact him. I wanted to find out for myself what kind of man he really was.

I wasn't sure what was going on with the guys. They were getting louder by the minute, and I could tell they were upset about something. Sheppard's voice was rising, and his fists were clenched at his side. I got curious, so I walked over closer to them. I started picking up empty beer bottles so I could listen to what they were saying.

"The fucker was doing the exchange in broad daylight man. It didn't even faze him when I drove by," Sheppard shouted.

"These fucking idiots are just asking for trouble," Otis barked.

"Did you tell Bishop about it?" Doc asked Sheppard.

"Yeah. He said Crack Nut had some new leads. He's looking into them, and they'll call us for a meet when they know more."

I had no idea what they were talking about, so I decided it was a good time to go check on John Warren. I eased the door open and peeked inside. He was sound asleep in his new crib, and Melinda was laying on the bed reading a book.

"He's doing fine, sweetie. You don't have to worry about that little guy. He's handling things just fine," Melinda said in her motherly voice. I really liked her. She reminded me a lot of Tessa's mother. Soft spoken but always made her point.

"Thanks for watching him, Melinda. I know he's in good hands with you," I told her.

"Are the boys giving you a hard time?" she asked.

"They're all pretty tense tonight. I think something's going on."

"Yeah, Doc said there's a new club trying to stake claim in town, and they're worried about it," she said with concern in her voice.

"They seem pretty pissed."

"Bishop has worked hard to get the club in a good place. They don't want anyone coming around messing things up, so they're a little on edge."

"That explains a lot. I guess they're trying to drink it off their minds," I said.

"It shouldn't be long, dear, especially at the rate they're going," she said laughing.

I hoped she was right. I'd had just about all I could

take of the tension in the bar. At least they weren't taking it out on me. They seemed to get that I wasn't there for them to give a hard time. I appreciated that. Too bad they didn't feel the same way about each other.

I was relieved when they all decided to call it a night. Sheppard was the last one to leave, and he reminded me to lock the door behind him. As I locked the door, I hoped that Goliath had a key. I knew it was late, but a part of me hoped that he would make it back sometime that night. I decided not to use the dead bolt just in case.

I sent Melinda home and got ready for bed. I took off my jeans and pulled on an old t-shirt to sleep in. I slipped into bed and pulled the covers over me. It was a little cold, but I liked it that way. I looked over at the crib, and John Warren was still sound asleep. It was nice having him there with me. It meant a lot to me that Melinda stayed with him. I'd have to find a way to pay her back sometime.

I was just about to drift off to sleep when I heard footsteps walking down the hall. I could hear male voices, but I couldn't make out what they were saying. I jumped out of bed and gently opened the door just enough for me to see that Goliath was talking to Bulldog. They must have just gotten back. I looked over at the clock and saw it was 2 a.m. I looked back through the crack of the door just in time to see Goliath go into his room and shut the door. My heart raced just knowing that he was so close to me.

I got back in bed and tried to settle my nerves. I laid there for a few minutes and realized it wasn't working. I couldn't stop thinking about him. I needed to see him, to touch him. I knew I wouldn't be able to sleep until I did, so I eased myself out of bed, being careful not to wake up John Warren. I left the door open just in case and quietly slipped down the hall.

My nerves were going wild as I stood in front of his door. I had no idea what I was doing there, but I couldn't pull myself away. Just when I was about to lose my nerve, I lifted my hand to the door and knocked lightly. I was freaking out. My heart was beating a mile a minute, and I couldn't decide if I should just turn around and go back to my room, or wait for him to open the door. I was about to forget the whole thing when Goliath appeared, his lips curled into a sexy smile, wearing nothing but a pair of boxers. I took a deep breath as my eyes roamed over the tattoos on his bare chest. Damn, the man was perfect. I stood there for what seemed like hours before Goliath reached for my hand, pulling me into his arms.

I rested my head on his chest and whispered, "I missed you."

"You have time to figure things out?" he asked. He knew the answer to that. I wouldn't have been there if I hadn't.

"Yes," I whispered as his arms hugged me tighter. He held me close against his chest, and I could feel his heart beat against my temple. The smell of his cologne surrounded me as my hands ran up and down his back. I loved how safe I felt in his arms. I could've stood in that moment for eternity. Even with the warmth of his touch, my body shivered from the coldness of the room. He pulled free from our embrace and ran his hands down my arms.

"Damn... you're freezing," he said lifting me in his arms. He gently cradled my legs in his arms and carried me over to his bed. He carefully rested me on the bed and laid down beside me. Once he pulled the covers over us, he pulled me over to him. I rested my head on his chest as my fingers roamed over the lines of his tattoo.

"Where's Little Man?" he asked.

"Next door, in Ace's old room. I left the door open so I could hear him."

"Okay," he whispered as he gently ran his fingers through my hair. I smiled against his chest. It meant so much to me that he cared about John Warren.

"I don't like it when you're gone," I told him. "I know it sounds crazy, but I miss you driving me nuts. It's like part of me is missing. That's crazy, right?"

"Not crazy, Lily. If that's the way you feel, it isn't the least bit crazy," he told me as he played with a strand of my hair.

"Did you have a good trip?" I asked.

"Don't wanna talk about work, babe. I've got you in my bed, in my arms, and that's all I wanna think about." His voice was deep and filled with promise. I should've felt content just having him close to me, but I wanted more.

"Goliath? Can I ask you something?"

"Anything."

"What's your real name?" It didn't really matter. He

would always be Goliath to me, but I wanted to know more about him.

"Colt. Colton Hayes."

"Really? I didn't expect a name like Colton. Maybe... Sterling or Remington. Colton seems kind of tame for someone like you." I could feel his laugh as it vibrated through his chest. I liked the sound of his laugh.

"I haven't been Colton for a very long time," he replied.

"Well, I like it. Colton, Colt, or Goliath. It doesn't matter to me," I said as I pulled myself up on my knees. I lifted my leg over his waist, so I was straddling him. I rested my hands on his chest as I looked down on him.

"Lily..." he stammered. I didn't give him a chance to protest. I leaned over him, pressing my lips to his. Without any further hesitation, his hands reached up and grabbed me by the back of my hair taking control of the kiss. When his tongue brushed against mine, I felt a surge of heat soar through my body. I'd never felt such a strong desire for a man. He was consuming me, filling me with want. Sensing my need for more, his hands released my hair and moved down my body to my thighs. His fingers dug into my skin as he guided me over his erection, rocking me back and forth against his hard cock. His growl of approval filled the room. I continued to grind into him as he slowly moved his hands to the hem of my shirt. He pulled my shirt over my head, exposing my bare breasts. He let out a deep breath as he took my breasts in his hands, holding them firmly as his thumb brushed across my nipple. I felt his erection throbbing beneath me, and I wanted to have him inside me. A hiss escaped his lips as I reached down, slipping the tips of my fingers into his boxers. Just as I wrapped my fingers around him, my attention was drawn to a desperate cry coming from down the hallway. Panic surged through me as I realized it was John Warren. I quickly reached for my t-shirt, throwing it over my head.

"Shit. Shit. Shit. I'm so, so sorry," I cursed as I jumped out of the bed. I continued to whisper, "I'm so sorry" under my breath as I left his room and headed down the hall. I could hear the springs on the bed squeak as he got out of the bed to follow me. John Warren had big tears streaming down his face by the time I reached the crib. I lifted him up into my arms, cradling him close to my chest. As soon as his head fell on my shoulder, he stopped crying. Something must have scared him. I was swaying side to side trying to get him to fall back asleep when I noticed Goliath standing in the doorway watching us.

CHAPTER 14

GOLIATH

"**I** 'M SO SORRY, Goliath. I don't know what I was thinking," she said with worry in her voice.

"Don't do that. There's nothing to be sorry about," I told her. Things like this were going to happen, and she was gonna need to get used to it.

"You... you aren't mad about this?" she said looking surprised by my words.

"Nothing to be mad about Lily." Damn, the girl was beautiful. My chest tightened seeing her standing there, still carrying the taste of her on my lips. My heart was all twisted up in knots, and I knew right then, in that very moment, I would do anything for her. I walked over to her and placed my hand on JW's little head. His eyes were closed, and it looked like he had already fallen back to sleep. She looked down at him and smiled. The love she had for him radiated throughout the room. She may not have been his mother, but you never would've known it by looking at her with him.

"It looks like he's fallen back asleep. You get him settled, and I'll see you in the morning," I told her. I leaned over and lightly kissed her forehead before I turned for the door.

"Goliath?" she called.

I turned back just as she was laying him in the crib. Once she had him settled, she walked over to me. She placed the palms of her hands on my chest and lifted herself up on her tiptoes, kissing me lightly on the lips. "Thank you," she whispered.

I couldn't help myself. I wrapped my arms around her waist and pulled her hard against my chest taking her mouth in a deep kiss. I loved how her body felt against my bare skin. I wanted to take her right then and there, but I knew it wasn't the right time or place. I released her quickly before I had a chance to change my mind. "Goodnight, Lil'. Get some sleep. I have big plans for you tomorrow."

Her brows furrowed and I knew she wondered what I meant, but I didn't plan on sharing what I had in mind. I wanted to surprise her, so I left before she could ask any questions. I heard her door click shut just as I entered my room. I took a deep breath enjoying her scent that still lingered in the air. It'd been a long time since I'd had something to look forward to, and I was definitely looking forward to spending the day with her. I knew I wouldn't have any trouble sleeping that night. I crawled back into bed and closed my eyes, thinking of what I would need to do to make the next day perfect.

Lily and JW were still asleep when I got up, so I got busy making some calls. I called Crack Nut Bobby first. I needed Courtney to watch JW for a little while. After I told him what I had in mind, Bobby told me it wouldn't be a problem. They said they'd be by to pick him up in an hour.

With everything lined up, I needed to get Lily and JW up and ready for the day. I tapped on her door, but she didn't answer. I knocked a little louder but still nothing. I turned the knob and found it wasn't locked. I eased the door open and saw JW still sleeping in his crib. The bed was empty, but I could hear the shower running in the bathroom. I figured I'd give her time to finish getting ready and come back in a few minutes.

As soon as I tried to shut the door, JW rolled over and stared at me. A smile spread across his little face as he rubbed his eyes with his little fist. He reached out his hands asking for me to pick him up. I couldn't have resisted that face if I'd tried. I leaned over the crib pulling him up to my chest. He pulled on the collar of my shirt and started babbling. It cracked me up that he was trying to talk to me.

"Dude, you need a diaper change. You stink," I told him. I reached over to the diaper bag by Lily's bed and looked for everything I'd need. I laid him on the bed and got to work changing him. He continued to babble and giggle as I took the old diaper off him. I had him ready to go by the time Lily walked back into the room. She had a small towel wrapped around her, and water was dripping from her hair.

I lifted JW into my arms and said, "I got him. You finish getting ready, and we'll meet you in the kitchen."

"Okay," she said hesitantly.

"Where's his food?" I asked.

"There's some in the bag, but I... uh..." she paused, and then a smile slowly crossed her face before she continued. "I don't have a high chair here."

"I'll make do," I told her. I would add another high chair to my list of things for the new prospects to take care of. There was no way I was gonna make a habit of feeding that kid on my lap.

When I got in the kitchen, Melinda was making a big breakfast for Doc and Sheppard. Her eyes lit up the minute she saw JW.

"There's my new favorite guy," she said reaching for JW. Doc shook his head and smiled. Their kids had already grown-up and gone, but she still had that motherly touch. She reached out and took the baby jars from my hand.

"I have him. You grab a plate and eat," she ordered. I loaded my plate and sat with the guys.

"You on baby patrol today?" Doc asked.

"Just for a bit. Lily's getting dressed, and then I'm taking her out for the day. I have Courtney coming to get JW while we're gone."

"You didn't have to do that. I would have loved to watch him," Melinda said as she sat him in her lap. She fed him several bites and didn't get a drop of baby food on her. The lady was a pro.

"I thought you'd want a break after last night, but I'm sure you'll have another date with him soon enough."

"I hope so. I need to talk to Tessa and make sure she

has me on that calendar of hers," she said laughing.

I turned to Sheppard and asked, "What about the new prospects?"

"They came last night. Just got back from their last deployment. They're out in the garage getting acquainted with everything," Sheppard replied.

"Good. Looking forward to meeting them," I told him. With the new club moving in on our territory, it'd be nice to have more members in the club. These guys were military, so they'd know how to handle themselves. I had some things for them to take care of, so I'd have to stop by the garage before we left.

Lily walked in wearing a pair of loose fit jeans with worn out knees and a Tennessee Vols long sleeve t-shirt. She'd pulled her hair up into a ponytail, and she wore just enough makeup to make the color of her eyes seem darker.

"Come grab some breakfast," I told her, motioning to the seat beside me.

"Melinda, this looks amazing! I'm starving," she said as she filled her plate with bacon and eggs.

"Thanks, hon. JW was pretty hungry, too. He just finished off his second jar of peaches," Melinda explained.

"So, *big guy*… whatcha got planned for us today?" Lily asked me smiling wide.

"It's a surprise, but you'll need a good jacket and your boots. We'll run by your place before we head out."

"What about JW?" she asked.

"Taken care of. Now, eat so we can head out."

"Mmm, okay…." She seemed a little hesitant to trust me, but she went with it. That pleased me. Maybe she was figuring things out after all.

I told Lily I would be right back. It was time I met the new prospects Sheppard had brought in. Bishop was showing them all the things they needed to take care of in the garage when I walked up.

He looked over to me and said, "Goliath, meet Conner and Levi." They both reached out their hand to me as Bishop said, "Goliath is our VP. He'll keep you posted on the things that you need to know. If he tells you to do something, do it. No questions asked."

They both nodded their heads. Nothing like new prospects – so eager to please. They were both pretty big guys, and they were still sporting their military haircuts – high and tight. It was going to be good to have them around. I didn't have time to waste on small talk, so I told them all the things I needed them to do. They listened to everything and didn't even ask a question when I told them I needed them to pick up a Christmas tree. I figured that was a good sign, so I gave them Lily's address and headed back inside. I had a big day planned, and it was time to get going.

Once Courtney got there to pick up JW, we were set to go. Lily followed me outside to my bike but stopped when I got on and started the engine.

I handed her a helmet and nodded my head for her to get on. She stood there a moment, and then a huge grin spread across her face. She stepped forward, taking the helmet out of my hands. She quickly slipped it on and buckled it. She threw her leg over the bike and wrapped her arms around my waist. I'd heard her say that she used to ride with her dad, but I was still impressed that she seemed to know what she was doing. She scooted up, pressing her breasts into my back, and shouted, "Ready!" My girl was excited, and I liked it.

When I pulled into her driveway, she quickly jumped off and raced up to her porch. She turned back to me and said, "I'll be right back!"

She quickly returned wearing her black boots, and a heavy black jacket with matching gloves. It wasn't leather, but it would do for today. I couldn't stop myself from thinking about her wearing a leather jacket bearing my name. She eased herself back on the bike and resumed her previous position. She tapped me on the back letting me know she was ready. Yeah, she definitely knew what she was doing.

I really didn't have a destination in mind. I just wanted to spend the day with her on my bike. I took her out by the lake, stopping by some of my favorite spots. Her nose was bright red from the chill of the day, but she didn't seemed fazed by it. She was eager to go anywhere I wanted to take her. We rode for several hours before we made our first stop. Her arms hugged me tighter when I pulled into the old Christmas tree farm. As soon as I killed the engine, she started with the questions.

"What are we doing here?"

"I'd think that was pretty obvious."

"Are you getting a Christmas tree?" she asked.

"No... *you're* getting a Christmas tree."

"How much is a real Christmas tree?"

"Don't know. Don't care," I said firmly. I was getting her a tree. It was JW's first Christmas, and I wanted him to have the best tree we could find.

"I doubt I can afford this," she said looking down at her feet.

I didn't want to argue with her, but I'd already made up my mind. I grabbed her hand and pulled her through the main gates of the tree farm.

"Goliath… I…." she said pulling her hand from mine.

"Lily, don't make a big deal about this. I know you have a hard time letting people do stuff like this for you, but I'm gonna get you a tree today."

She looked like she was getting pissed, so I continued, "Look, it's been a long time since I've actually looked forward to Christmas. Don't give me a hard time."

She thought about for a minute before she reached for my hand and simply said, "Okay."

We walked around the farm for over an hour before I found the perfect tree. It was a thick spruce just over 7 feet tall. I paid the owner and told him that Conner and Levi would be by later to pick it up. We got back on the bike and headed for the store, so we could buy a couple boxes of lights and some ornaments.

Once we had everything we needed, we stopped by the local Italian restaurant to pick up dinner. When we pulled up in Lily's driveway, I was relieved to see that the prospects had actually followed through. They'd put the

Christmas tree and a few boxes of extra ornaments on the front porch just like I'd asked. I was impressed. They even remembered to get the popcorn. My dad would always get us to help him make a popcorn garland to go around our tree, and I thought it would be cool to do it again with Lily. As soon as we finished our dinner, we decided to get started on the tree.

"Where do you want to put it?" I asked.

"How about in front of the window so people can see it when they drive by," Lily said sounding excited.

"You go make the popcorn while I set everything up. Crack Nut texted me and said they were on their way with JW."

"Great. I'll get started," she stood there watching me pull the tree in from the porch. "Thank you," she whispered. Sweet Lily was hard to resist. I walked over to her and put my hands on her hips, pulling her close to me.

I leaned over her and lightly kissed the side of her neck. I felt a shiver vibrate through her body as I continued kissing her along her jaw. When I found my way to her lips, she wrapped her arms around my neck and reached for the edges of my hair. Her tongue brushed against mine, and I claimed her mouth with a deep, demanding kiss. I wanted her more in that moment than I ever thought possible. Her nails dug into my neck as I lifted her legs up around my waist. I knew she felt how hard I was for her when she began to grind her hips into mine. I turned us towards the hallway to her bedroom. My heart stopped cold when I heard the knock on the door. Damn! I released her from the kiss and eased her down to the floor. I could see the lust in her eyes when I leaned over and kissed her on the forehead.

"Crack Nut never has been one to have good timing," I told her as I went for the door.

"I don't think it's possible for me to be any more sexually frustrated than I am right now," Lily said with disappointment.

"Is that right? I think I'll take that as a challenge," I told her laughing as I opened the door. Bobby was standing at the door with JW on his hip and his diaper bag hanging over his shoulder.

"Hey, Bobby. How'd he do?" Lily asked as she walked past me to take JW.

"Great. I didn't think Courtney was ever gonna let me bring him back. She's crazy about that kid."

"Thanks for helping me out today," I told him.

"Anytime. We would have kept him longer, but I'm taking Court to see that new movie with that creepy doll. She's all excited about it."

"I've been wanting to see that. Tell Courtney to call me tomorrow, so she can tell me all about it," Lily said as she took JW into the kitchen.

"By the way, thought I'd let you know, I think I found the warehouse they're using. It's actually an old shop a guy built for his farm equipment. Someone offered him double the asking price, and they paid cash."

"Yeah, that sounds like what we're looking for. Did you get a name?" I asked.

"No. Figured it'd be made up anyway."

"No doubt."

"I better get going. I think John Warren's pretty wiped, man. Courtney played with him the whole time, and he never took a nap."

"That works out just fine. Thanks, and y'all have fun tonight. Never been a big fan of those damn scary movies," I told him.

"I guess we'll see what all the fuss is about tonight. Catch ya later," Bobby said as he turned to leave. I shut the door just as Lily walked back in with JW and his bottle.

"I think he's ready for bed. I'm going to change him and put him down. I'll be back in a minute."

"I'll finish setting things up. Take your time," I told her as she headed down the hall.

Getting the tree in that stupid stand was harder than I thought. It kept leaning to the left, so I had to keep working with the damn thing until I got it straight. I finally had it set up when Lily came back in. The edges of her lips curled into a bright smile as she looked at the tree.

"It's perfect," she said with wonder in her voice.

"Yeah, it kinda is."

"So, what's next?" she asked.

"I'll fight the lights while you make the popcorn."

"You got it!" she said running for the kitchen.

The entire house smelled like popcorn by the time she finished. I was still stringing up the lights when she walked in with a huge bowl of popcorn and the needle and thread. I kept working while she made herself a spot on the floor. I watched her for a minute and realized she was stringing it wrong. There was no way it would stay on the string the way she was doing it.

"Lily, have you ever done that before?" I asked.

"Nope."

"I can tell," I told her.

Her eyebrows shot up, and before I had time to move, she threw a handful of popcorn right in my face. When she noticed my surprise, she started laughing hysterically.

"You are so gonna pay for that shit, *little girl*," I told her as I grabbed the bowl from her hands. I took a handful of popcorn and grabbed the back of her shirt, stuffing it full. She jumped up and pulled her shirt out of the back of her pants, releasing it all onto the floor.

"That's not fair!" she shouted, reaching for the bowl. I lifted it over my head, keeping it out of her reach.

"You asked for it."

She stopped reaching for the bowl and grabbed a handful of popcorn from the floor. She caught me off guard as she shoved her hand down the front of my pants. Pulling her hand out, she released the popcorn to fall down my jeans. She put her hands on her hips and stared at me with a smirk.

"You just took this to a whole new level, little girl," I scowled. She realized that she was about to get it big time, so she turned and tried to run from me. I grabbed her by the waist, pulling her back against my chest.

"I'm sorry…. Really! I didn't mean to do it!" she

gasped, shaking her head from side to side. She was laughing, but I could hear the panic in her voice.

"You meant to do it, and now you're gonna pay for it," I told her as I grabbed another handful of popcorn. I held it out in front of her taunting her, and asked, "You decide…. Where do you want it?" I was trying to fight back my smile, but I was having too much fun.

"Goliath, don't!" she pleaded.

"Decide," I said trying to sound forceful.

Her expression suddenly changed from panicked to something else entirely. A wicked grin crossed her face as she said, "Okay, then…think about what you want me to take off first, and… put it there."

Her boldness surprised me, but damn if I didn't like it. I dropped the bowl on the coffee table and let the popcorn fall from my hands. I put both hands on her hips and pulled her closer to me. Her back was pressed firmly against my chest, and I had no doubt that she could feel just how hard she made me.

I leaned over and whispered into her ear, "You know, there are all kinds of ways I can punish you, *little girl.*"

CHAPTER 15

LILY

———◦◦◦———

I COULD FEEL the goosebumps prickle over my skin as he whispered in my ear. Excitement coursed through me when I thought about all the brilliant ways he could torture me with his body. An electric charge surged through me as I felt his erection press into my back. I squeezed my thighs together to try to ease the throbbing between my legs when he mentioned punishing me. I had no idea what he meant, but my arousal outweighed any worries or doubt.

"Show me," I told him, urging him on.

The bristles of his day old beard raked across my neck as he nipped at my ear. "Eager Lily wants to be punished, doesn't she?" he asked as his fingers dug into my sides. He began licking and nipping the side of my neck, and I tried to turn to face him, but he held me in place. He continued to kiss my neck while he reached for the hem of my shirt. I only lost his mouth long enough for him to pull my shirt over my head. He tossed it to the ground and continued to place light kisses all over my neck and shoulder. I wanted his mouth, so I quickly turned towards him, hoping he wouldn't stop me again.

I wrapped my arms around his neck pulling him down to me and placed my lips on his. My nails dug into his back as I moaned into his mouth. He never broke the kiss as he lifted me into his arms and carried me down the hall. He pushed my bedroom door open and walked over to the bed. He laid me down on my back and then quickly removed my boots and jeans. He stood over me, staring with want in his eyes, as I lay there in just my black bra and panties.

"Fuck... you're amazing," he said in almost a whisper. "Not gonna be able to wait, Lily. I gotta have you. Now."

I didn't want him to wait. I couldn't imagine wanting anything more in my life. "Please..." I pleaded.

I watched in wonder as he began removing his clothes. I loved the way his muscles rippled as he bent down to remove his jeans and boxers. He stood there in all his glory, allowing my eyes to roam over his beautiful body. I lifted myself up on my elbows so I could get a good look at him. He was perfect. He had a large tattoo covering one arm and another one on his abdomen. I'd always known that he was a large man, but that was more than I could take. I was tired of waiting for him to come to me, so I pulled myself up on my knees and moved to the edge of the bed. I slipped my hands around his waist trying to pull him closer to me. He didn't budge.

"Goliath?"

"I don't want to hurt you, Lily, but I don't have it in me to go slow right now. I want to give you what you need," he said firmly.

"I don't *want* you to go slow," I told him truthfully. I pulled my arms away from him and reached behind my back to remove my bra. My eyes never left his as I let it drop to the floor. Both of his hands reached behind my neck, grabbing my hair firmly as he began kissing me deeply. In a matter of seconds, I was lying flat on my back with the weight of his body pressed against me. I felt my underwear tug at my flesh as he ripped them from my body. The warmth of his breath caressed my neck as I raked my nails against the hard muscles of his back. My hips shifted towards him as his cock rubbed against my entrance. My entire body ached for him to the point that I was losing control. I desperately wanted him inside me.

"Please... Goliath. Now," I urged.

"I'm going to take you hard and fast, Lily."

He reached out and took the condom from his jeans. He slid it down his long shaft and then rested himself back between my thighs. I wrapped my legs around his waist, rocking against him, hoping he would finally give me what I so desperately needed. A thunderous growl vibrated through his chest as my teeth nipped at his neck.

"You ready for me?" he asked as he reached between us, searching for the answer. His fingers entered me, brushing back and forth over the spot that drove me crazy. A moan escaped my lips as he delved deeper inside me.

"Yes. Please."

Just when I thought I couldn't take it a moment longer, he thrust deep inside me, giving me all he had to give. He stopped for a moment to give me time to adjust and asked, "You okay?"

"God, yes. Don't stop!"

His hands reached up to the nape of my neck, fisting my hair as he began thrusting into me. Each move was more demanding than the last. His teeth raked over my nipples, and I cried out wanting more. I dug my nails into his back as my whole body became ignited with such an intense heat I thought I wouldn't survive it. He pushed deeper inside me as I tightened around him. A deep growl of pleasure vibrated in his throat as he continued to pound into my flesh. I fought to catch my breath as I felt my climax approaching. My entire body jolted and jerked as my orgasm took hold. I continued to tighten around his throbbing cock until he found his own release. His body collapsed on top of mine, exhausted and sweaty. I loved how he felt pressed against my bare skin, buried deep inside me. I never wanted to leave that spot.

Goliath's breathing began to settle, and he slowly began to lift some of his weight off of me. I kept my legs wrapped around his waist, not wanting him to go too far.

"Don't go," I told him.

"I'll be back. I'm not done with you yet," he whispered. "Don't move," he commanded as he lifted himself off the bed.

Excitement washed over me when I thought of the possibility of having him again so soon. I laid there sprawled out on the bed, waiting for him to return. All my inhibitions were completely thrown out the window. I wanted anything this man had to give me. No more fighting it. No more worrying if it was right or wrong. It was done. I'd fallen for the biker. I watched him walk back into the room, his erection growing with every step he took. I never moved. I couldn't. I was totally lost in him.

He lowered himself down between my legs and began kissing along the curve of my breast. He looked up to me and said, "Lil, I'm going to fuck you slow. Real slow... and you're going to love every minute of it."

"Mmm, yes," I hissed as he took my nipple in his mouth.

"I don't think I'll ever get enough of you," he whispered. I felt the same way. Every move he made was slow and deliberate. His hands roamed gently over my entire body, leaving traces of burning need with each touch. He took his time getting acquainted with every inch of my body, torturing me with his mouth and hands. I let my fingers trace over the contours of his rigid body, loving how he responded to my touch. Even when I was at the brink of pure exhaustion, I continued to want more of him. My muscles trembled, my heart raced, but I couldn't get enough. I knew I desperately needed sleep, but I didn't want to miss a minute of what he had to give me. His words, *I don't think I'll ever get enough of you*, drifted through my thoughts as he showed me how much he truly meant it, over and over, until the sun came up the next morning.

CHAPTER 16

GOLIATH

I KEPT LILY up for most of the night, so I decided to
let her sleep in. I didn't know how she ever got any
sleep on that damn mattress. I knew she wasn't gonna
like it, but she was getting a new one as soon as possible.
There was no way I could keep sleeping on that damn
thing.

When JW woke up crying, I carefully shut her door
and went to his room to get him. As soon as he saw me,
his crying stopped. He was obviously surprised to see
me. I tried to be quiet as I changed his diaper and put on
his clothes. I wanted Lily to get the rest that she needed.

After I fed him some oatmeal, I brought him into the
living room so I could finish putting the lights on the
tree. First, I had to clean up the huge mess we'd made
with the popcorn so JW would stop trying to shove it in
his mouth. He watched with fascination as I swept
everything into a big pile and threw it into the garbage.
He sat on the floor beside me, so I could keep an eye on
him while I worked. He finally gave up on the popcorn
and grabbed his new football to shove into his mouth.

"Dude, we already talked about that. Footballs are for throwing, not chewing." Drool started to slip out of his mouth as he kept gnawing at the damn thing. "You're killing me, Little Man," I told him laughing. Damn, the kid was cute.

I finished putting up all the lights on the tree and decided it was time to make Lily some coffee. I was just about to pour her a cup when she walked into the kitchen. She was wearing that same tiny bathrobe she'd worn before. This time, though, she wasn't trying to hide behind the damn thing, and I liked it.

"Morning, sleepyhead. You want some coffee?" I asked.

"I'd love some," she said pulling out a chair from the kitchen table. "How long have you been up?"

"Awhile," I told her as I handed her the cup of coffee.

"Looks like you've been busy," she said nodding her head towards the living room.

"I wanted to have it done before I left today." I hated the thought of leaving her after the night we'd shared, but I had to get to the garage today. We had to get those jobs done, or Bishop was going to lose his shit.

"The tree looks great. I can't wait to see it with the ornaments on it. Will you come back by later tonight when it's finished?" she asked looking up at me.

"I'd like that." I walked over to her and leaned down giving her a brief kiss on the lips. "I better get going."

Before I had a chance to move, she quickly stood up and wrapped her arms around my waist. She rested her head on my chest and said, "Thank you for last night. I had a great time, and I really love the tree."

She felt so good in my arms, like she was meant to be there. "I had a good time, too, Lil'. I'll be back later tonight."

She lifted her head to look at me, and I kissed her once more. This time, the kiss was not brief. I took my time memorizing the feel of her lips, the taste of her mouth. I wanted to carry that memory with me. This kiss was long and intense, and it was full of promise.

"I'll see you tonight," I told her as I headed out the door. It was nice having something to look forward to. I had no doubt that it was going to be a pain in the ass to get all those orders done in time. It was important for the club, so we couldn't be late. Since we decided to stop running drugs, the garage had been the only thing keeping our club going. Bishop wanted us to have something our brothers could be proud of, so he decided to stop all illegal activity. Looking back, I think it was the best decision we ever made.

When I got to the garage, Renegade and Sheppard were already working on the two cars we'd brought back from Texas. Bulldog was busy working on the 1969 Chevy Impala we were supposed to get up and running. He'd already taken the carburetor out and was cleaning it when I walked up.

"Dude, you're late," Bulldog huffed.

"I got held up," I said laughing him off. He rolled his eyes and grinned. He knew where I was, so there was no need in trying to explain.

We spent the next eight hours taking that old, rusted engine apart and cleaning every little nut and bolt. When we finally had the damn thing put back together, Bulldog climbed in the cab and tried to start it up. The garage filled with hoots and hollers when the old beauty cranked on the first try. Bulldog's face lit up with pride when the other guys came over to check out our work. That was what it was all about. I loved spending time with my brothers like that. It was the best part of being VP of the club.

It was around 7 o'clock when we finished up in the garage, so I ran by my room at the clubhouse to take a shower. Just as I was finishing putting on my boots, someone knocked on the door. I opened it to see Bishop standing there.

"You got a minute?" he asked.

"Yeah, what's up?" I asked motioning for him to come in. He had a troubled look on his face as he made his way into my bedroom. I figured he wanted to talk about the issues with the new club, so I closed the door and waited for him to speak.

"We need to talk about Lily." My gut twisted the minute he spoke her name. I clenched my fists knowing he wouldn't come to me like that unless there was trouble.

"What the hell is going on?" I asked. I could feel my heart pounding in my chest as I waited for him to explain.

"Tessa and I were talking, and some things she said made me think it's time we look into JW's dad. Something isn't right, and I want to know what it is. Tessa said she mentioned something about keeping Little Man safe from his dad. I don't like the fucking sound of that."

"Shit. Sheppard mentioned something to me a few weeks ago about it, but I've been…."

"Distracted," Bishop snapped.

"Yes, I've been focused on *other* things," I admitted.

"Tessa said the father's name is Maverick, and he's a member of Satan's Fury, a small MC in Washington. I'm going to have Crack Nut look into them," Bishop told me.

"I'll talk to Lily. I'll find out what I can from her."

"Good. I don't want trouble with these guys, but I consider Lily to be one of our own now. They fuck with her, they fuck with us," Bishop growled. I knew he was concerned about the trouble it could bring our club. We already had other issues with the new club to deal with, but it meant a lot to me that he was still willing to do what it took to keep Lily safe.

"You think these guys will really come looking for them?" I asked.

"I have no idea, but I'm not gonna risk it." He got up and headed towards the door. He stopped when we were face to face and placed his hand on my shoulder. "Keep an eye on Lily. I don't want anything happening to her or the baby."

"You know I will." I looked Bishop in the eye and said, "She's it for me, man. No way in hell I'll ever let anyone hurt her. She's mine, and I'll protect her and JW."

I didn't waste any time getting over to Lily's house. The lights from the Christmas tree were shining through the front window when I pulled up in the driveway. I had to smile. It looked pretty damn good all lit up like that. She had the tree all decorated, and she'd even put a wreath on the front door.

Lily rushed out to meet me on the front porch with a bright smile and said, "What do you think?"

"It looks great, Lil'." I took a moment to look at everything she had done. It really did look great.

She lifted up on her tiptoes to kiss me on the lips, then said, "Come in and check out the tree!" She tucked her arm through mine and pulled me into the living room. It was nice to see her so excited, but I needed to find out what was going on.

"Lily, we need to talk," I said firmly.

"Well, damn… that doesn't sound good." She gave me a serious look and then walked over to the sofa. She sat down and motioned to the seat next to her, encouraging me to sit.

As soon as my ass hit the seat, she blurted out, "Spill it." She looked at me with her eyebrow raised high and her back perched straight.

I cleared my throat and said, "We need to talk about JW." A surprised look crossed her face. Her nails dug into her knee caps as she started biting her lower lip. She looked down to the floor and took a deep breath. I knew then she had secrets, secrets she might not have been ready to share. "Lily, you can trust me."

"It's not that I don't trust you, Goliath. I just haven't

really wanted to think about it lately. Everything's been going great, and I'm scared that if I think about it or talk about it, something bad will happen."

"I won't let anything happen to either of you. You gotta know that. But I need to know what's going on, so I can keep you safe."

Lily spent the next hour explaining everything that had happened the day her mother brought JW to her house. She was obviously upset about the loss of her sister, and she'd do anything to protect her nephew. I respected her for that. I thought it was pretty shitty the way her mother had handled things, but Lily was tough and had made the best of it.

"Bishop and I are going to have Bobby look into Maverick and his club. I need to know what we're dealing with," I told her.

"No, Goliath. I don't want the club to get involved. It's not their problem."

"You and JW will be taken care of, Lily. You're a part of this club, and we protect our own."

"I don't want anyone to get hurt. Just please… be *careful*," Lily said as she put her hand on my knee.

"Always. You got any other secrets I need to know about?" I asked with a smile. I figured she'd told me everything, but I was wrong.

"I wouldn't call them secrets exactly," Lily said. "It's just… I've been thinking about calling my dad."

"Why wouldn't you call him?" I asked.

"My mother wasn't a big fan of bikers. She said they were nothing but trouble. I didn't believe her until I had a run-in with one of my dad's club members. I loved my dad, but that guy freaked me out. After that, I began to think Mom may have been right."

"What happened at your dad's club?" Goliath growled as he clenched his fists at his sides.

"One of the men came on to me. Tried to force himself on me. He didn't get that far, but it scared me. I panicked. I should've kicked him in the balls and ended it. I'm not even sure if dad knows what happened."

"Call him. He needs to know what happened," I told her.

"What if he hates me?" she asked.

"He won't. Call him."

CHAPTER 17

LILY

G OLIATH WAITED FOR me inside, while I went out on the front porch to call my father. He was right. My dad didn't hate me. Actually, he was thrilled to hear from me and wanted to plan a visit. I told him all about Hailey and JW. He wasn't surprised at all. He seemed to know more about that situation than he let on, but I didn't push. I still loved my father, and it meant so much to me to talk to him. He was so understanding about every-thing. He had no idea what had happened with Big Mike all those years ago. I could hear the anger in his voice when he told me he wanted to kill him, but he wouldn't get his chance. Apparently karma had already intervened, and the asshole had died in a motorcycle wreck.

Goliath was coming out of JW's room when I got back inside. "Is he okay?" I asked.

"Yeah, just checking in on him. How'd it go with your dad?" he asked.

I reached up and put my arms around his neck. I rested my forehead on his shoulder and said, "You were right. He doesn't hate me." I was so relieved. I missed him more than I'd realized, and I wanted him to be a part of my life.

"Knew he wouldn't."

"He was just like I remembered," I told him.

"Good, I'm glad you called."

I looked up and smiled. "You want to watch a movie or something?"

"Yeah, but I'm not watching one of those damn scary movies. You got something else?" he asked.

"You pick. There are lots of movies on the shelf by the TV."

He walked over and took his time looking through all the movies in my collection. There were only romance or horror movies to choose from, so I had no idea what he would pick. He turned to me with a devilish grin on his face as he turned around with a movie in his hand. He lifted the cover up so I could see that he'd found *Talladega Nights* with Will Ferrell. I had no idea where that movie came from, but he looked pretty pleased that he found it.

"It's a classic, baby," he said laughing as he walked towards my room. I heard him mumbling quotes from the movie as he walked down the hall. I slipped the movie into the DVD player, and he returned from my bedroom carrying my favorite fleece blanket and a pillow. He was already waiting for me on the sofa when I started the movie.

"You want some popcorn or a beer?" I asked.

"Nope. Just you," he said with a sexy grin. I walked over to him and sat down, tucking myself under his arm.

He pulled the cover over my legs and lightly kissed me on the side of my head. I loved sitting there with him like that. The last few weeks had definitely taken me on a wild ride, but I'd do it all over again just to be right there in that moment.

"A classic?" I asked looking over to him.

"You heard me."

"It's Will Ferrell, Goliath. It's not a classic." I told him as I nudged his rib cage with my elbow.

"You realize those are fightin' words, babe. You don't mess with Will."

"Is that right?" I asked laughing.

He raised his eyebrows and said, "You really wanna go there, little girl?" That only made me laugh harder. He was being so serious, and I just couldn't get control of myself.

"I think I do!" I was laughing hysterically when Goliath stood up and reached for me. I was caught off guard as he threw me over his shoulder and started storming down the hall. "Wait!" I shouted, pounding my fists on his back. "I didn't mean it! Will Ferrell is *amazing*! He should get an Oscar!" I heard a loud *WHAP* just as the sting started to spread across my ass. Shit! He'd just smacked me on my ass. "Goliath!"

"Best stop talking, Lil'. There's more where that came from," he said deviously. I could feel the vibration of his laugh through his chest as he carried me across the bedroom. When he reached the edge of my bed, he tossed me onto it. I looked up to him wondering what he was going to do next. His expression was blank as he reached for my calves and pulled my ass to the edge of the bed. With one quick tug, he removed my pants and tossed them to the floor.

The room was filled with silence as he slowly pulled off his t-shirt and pants. My eyes roamed over his beautiful body igniting my overwhelming need for him. I could've stared at him like that for hours, but he didn't give me the chance. Goliath knelt down between my legs, resting his knees on the floor beneath me. My legs began to tremble with anticipation as he lowered his head between my thighs. His fingers dug into me, pulling me closer to him. The feel of the bristles of his beard brushing against my skin made me catch my breath.

He took his time torturing me with his mouth before he found the exact spot he was looking for. I clawed at the sheets beside me as his tongue swept across my center. Trying to hold on as he tortured me, my hands finally found purchase in his hair, demanding, urging him to stay in the spot that I needed him most. I could feel my release gathering in my stomach, growing in intensity with every stroke of his tongue. As soon as he realized that I was close to reaching my climax, he thrust two fingers deep inside me, sending me completely over the edge. My body tensed all over as the pleasure of the moment overtook me. He kept moving his fingers deep inside me as he lifted his knees off the floor. With one quick motion, he removed his fingers and plunged his cock deep into my core, never giving me a chance to recover. I instantly felt the tension in my legs building as my second orgasm began to take hold. As he stood, my legs wrapped around his waist, driving him harder with each move he made. It was not tender, or sweet. It was mad, passionate, uncontrollable desire, and I loved it. I loved everything he had to give me. With each forceful stroke, he guided himself deeper inside. I couldn't hold back any longer. The relentless pounding never stopped as my legs tightened around him, finally reaching my climax. His fingers ground into my shoulders as he thrust his cock deep inside me, finding his own release. Sweat dripped from his brow as his body rested on top of mine. I hated that I hadn't thought to remove my shirt. I wanted to feel his bare skin against mine. I slowly raked my nails along his back as his breathing returned to normal. He rolled to the side pulling me with him, our legs dangling off the bed.

I looked over to him and laughed. I raised my eyebrow and said, "Just saying, that's not the best way to get me to stop talking trash about Will Ferrell."

CHAPTER 18

GOLIATH

L ILY NEVER STOPPED surprising me. I was afraid that I'd been too rough with her, but she was lying there next to me laughing. Laughing! I was uncomfortable as hell laying there with my feet off the bed, so I pulled us both back to the center of the bed. Once we're settled, she shifted her ass against my stomach and pulled my arm across her chest. Within a few seconds, she's sound asleep.

We spent the next few nights following pretty much the same routine. I spent my days working in the garage, and my nights in her bed. I did finally get her a new mattress. She didn't even give me a hard time about it. I think she was actually relieved to see me bring it home.

When she worked nights at the bar, we would stay in Ace's old room with JW. Being with Lily was the best part of my day. Just knowing she was there waiting for me each night, gave me something to look forward to when things got hectic at the garage. I never imagined things could be that good with a woman, and I didn't want anything to fuck it up. I needed to check in with

Crack Nut. He was working on his computer when I walked into his room. I asked to see what he'd found out about Maverick. He quickly pulled up several files, and I was surprised by what he found out.

"There's nothing," Bobby said flatly.

"What the hell do you mean? There has to be something," I demanded.

"Dude, the guy has no record. He doesn't have so much as a parking ticket. I thought Lily said he was in all sorts of trouble," Bobby questioned.

"That's what she said. Her mother told her all kinds of shit about him. What about his club? You got anything on them?" I asked.

"Same deal. They've had a few run-ins with the cops over drug trafficking, but it's all low scale. They aren't even under investigation by the DEA," Bobby said.

"Fuck! That doesn't make sense. Lily was totally freaked out when she talked about this guy, and you're telling me there's nothing to even worry about. Doesn't add up."

"I'll keep digging, but man, I just don't see it…. He looks like he could be one of us," Bobby said as he pulled his picture up on the screen. I knew you couldn't tell a damn thing by a picture, but the guy seemed pretty tame to me. A few tattoos on his left arm, but no other signs that he was even a goddamn biker. He had dark brown hair, and the same color green eyes as JW. Damn. I was surprised by how much he looked like him. An uneasy feeling crept up in my gut when I thought about him being JW's father. Something wasn't right, and I needed to find out what was going on.

"Keep looking. There has to be something," I told him.

"I'm on it," Bobby told me. I was turning for the door to leave when he said, "You know the girls are planning to go out tonight."

"Yeah, Lily's looking forward to it."

"Courtney, too. She's been talking about it all week."

"Hopefully, they'll stay out of trouble," I told him.

"Yeah, right. Trouble seems to follow these girls wherever they go. We might need to keep an eye on them," Bobby said smiling.

"You're probably right about that. I'll catch up with you later on tonight. Let me know if you find anything on Maverick," I said as I left the room. I needed to get back over to the garage. There was still had of lot of work to get finished before I could head home.

CHAPTER 19

LILY

COURTNEY WAS IN rare form, and I loved it. She'd had us rolling all night, and she was just getting started. There weren't many people at Matt's, but the ones who were had their eyes glued on Courtney the entire time we'd been there. Every time a new song came on, everyone in the bar turned to see what she was going to do next. I loved watching her dance. She was the life of the party, and everyone was drawn to her. We'd all had several drinks, and even Tessa was letting loose. Just as we were finishing up our fourth dance, Courtney started shouting for more drinks.

"Let's get another round," Courtney yelled heading back over to the bar.

Tessa leaned over to me and whispered, "There's no way I'm going to be able to keep up with her tonight." We both laughed as I nodded in agreement. We followed her back to our table to get our drinks.

"This is so much fun! We have to do this more often!" Taylor said before she took a drink of her beer. I'd enjoyed getting to know her better. She lit up every time

133

she talked about Renegade. It was obvious that she was crazy about him, even if he still left the toilet seat up.

"I've got some news," Tessa said with a huge grin on her face.

"News! Oh my god, you're pregnant!" Courtney shouted with her hands waving all around her head. I shook my head knowing that couldn't be it. Tessa had been drinking, and there was no way she'd do that if she were pregnant.

"No, Court, I'm not pregnant," Tessa said nudging her with her shoulder. "Bishop and I have decided to elope over Christmas break!" We were all thrilled to hear that they'd finally decided to get married. I never thought she was the type to fall for a biker, but Bishop was perfect for her and truly made her happy.

Once we all settled back into our seats, I turned to her and said, "I'm so glad to see you happy like this Tess. You deserve it more than anyone I know."

"Thanks, sweetie. I never dreamed my life would turn out like this. I just can't believe it. I'm happy – really, really happy."

"Bishop's pretty much perfect for you. We all knew this was coming. Now that we have you all taken care of, Tess…." Taylor began. She turned to me and smirked, "When are you going to tell us about this thing with you and Goliath? We've been waiting all night to hear about it."

"Umm… things are going good," I told her.

"Come on, Lily. You have to give us more than that!" Tessa said.

"I don't know what to say... I told myself a long time ago that I wasn't going to get involved with a biker. I've heard too many horror stories, and just decided it wasn't for me. Let's just say Goliath has changed my mind," I told them smiling. Goliath had changed my mind about a lot of things. I had fallen for him, biker or not, and there was nothing I could do to stop it now.

"He's totally yummy," Courtney slurred. "And he's so big. Oh god! ...Is he big... like *everywhere*?" We all burst out laughing. I just shook my head. There was no way I was going there with her.

I decided to change the subject so I asked Courtney, "What about you and Bobby?"

"Hell, isn't that the question of the hour!" she said rolling her eyes and slamming her hand on the table. "One minute he's great. There are times that I think that he loves me just as much as I love him. Then, without any notice, he starts acting all weird and distant. I just don't know anymore."

Tessa put her hand on her arm and said, "Just give it time. We all know he's crazy about you."

"Then, why hasn't he *claimed* me yet? I'm thinking it's just not gonna happen." She looked so lost and confused. I hated that I ever even brought it up. I decided it was time for a distraction, so I gave Taylor a wink and headed over to the DJ. I wasn't paying attention to where I was going, and I walked right into a huge wall of muscle. Before I had a chance to see who it was, arms wrapped around my waist, and I felt a soft kiss on my forehead. I looked up to see Goliath smiling down at me.

"Hey! What are you doing here?" I asked. The scent of his cologne swirled around me as my eyes roamed over his body. Damn, he looked good. His hair was brushed back, and he was wearing his black DC's leather jacket with faded jeans and boots.

"The guys wanted to make sure y'all were staying out of trouble," he said nodding his head over to Bishop, Bobby, and Renegade. They were all making their way over to our table. Courtney's face lit up the minute she saw Bobby coming towards her. He couldn't have timed that any better.

"No trouble. We've been good," I told him smiling. I was glad he was there. I liked spending time with the girls, but having him there made the night even better.

I was surprised when Elvis Presley's song, "Can't Help Falling in Love", started playing. I'd always had a thing for Elvis, and that song was one of my favorites. Goliath took my hand and led me out onto the dance floor. His arms slipped around my waist, and he pulled me close against his chest. He held me tight as I rested my head on his shoulder listening to the words of the song. I smiled to myself thinking it was the perfect song for us. It was like no one else was in the room as we swayed back and forth to the music. He was the only thing that mattered to me at that moment. I didn't want to let go of him when the song ended, but it was time to head back over to the group.

I smiled when I noticed each of the men standing beside their women, staking their claim. Courtney may not have had a DC jacket yet, but it was obvious that she was Bobby's girl. No doubt about it. We spent another hour talking and playing pool before Bishop told Tessa it was time to go. It was time for them to go relieve the babysitter.

"I think we better get going, too," I told Goliath. "I'm sure Melinda is ready for us to get back."

"Ready when you are." Truthfully, I was just ready to have Goliath to myself. I'd had a great time with the girls, but now I just wanted some time alone with him.

I told the girls goodbye and followed Goliath out to his bike. It was really cold outside, but I didn't mind. I wanted to ride with him on his bike. I needed to be close to him. He took off his jacket and helped me put it on.

"It's freezing out here, babe. This is gonna be a fast trip, so get on and hold on tight."

A thrill shot through me as I got on behind him. I slipped my arms around his waist and tried to prepare myself for the bitter cold. It had been such a great night. I couldn't remember a time when I had been so happy. Unfortunately, that was all about to change.

CHAPTER 20

GOLIATH

I T WAS AMAZING how much could change in one night, one moment. You think everything is going your way, and you're oblivious to the darkness that lurks around the corner. Then, in an instant, life comes crashing down on you, and you know you will never be the same. Memories of my father's death kept coming back to me as I stood in the hospital waiting room. I sat with Lily watching the people I loved the most try to put on a brave face as they waited to hear the news – good or bad.

Earlier, the nurse came to ask Lily all these absurd questions, and I lost it. We didn't have time for that shit. I wanted to know how he was, and the fucking paper-work could wait. I knew getting angry with the nurse wouldn't help, but I couldn't think straight. I was worried about him, and I couldn't stop thinking that it was my fault. If I'd been there instead of Courtney, it never would've happened.

Lily had had to work at the bar that night, and it was Courtney's turn to babysit. She loved babysitting JW and added herself to the calendar every chance she got. Lily said she'd even brought all these *Baby Einstein* videos for JW to watch. No idea what those are, but Lily seemed pretty excited about it. Courtney planned to watch JW at Lily's until it was time for him to go to bed, and then she was going to bring him over to the club. Melinda would take over, so Lily wouldn't have to worry about driving home. I had to work late in the garage, so I thought it was a good plan. I was wrong. So fucking wrong.

Lily was heartbroken. She'd been crying hysterically since we found out about the wreck. We weren't exactly sure what happened, but it looked like Courtney had hit a deer on the way to the clubhouse. It totaled her car. It flipped into a ravine, and it took the fire department using the Jaws of Life to get them out of the car. One of the men told me that he was shocked to find them still alive. Courtney and JW were rushed to the hospital, and we were waiting to hear how they were.

I looked over at Bobby, and my chest tightened as I saw the expression on his face. My brother was having a hard time, and I couldn't say I blamed him. I couldn't imagine how I would feel if it was Lily in the operating room. I watched the color in his face drain away when one of the doctors came out to talk to him earlier. He'd told Bobby that she had a great deal of internal bleeding and needed emergency surgery. It would be several hours before we knew anything.

Lily jumped out of my arms and rushed to the doorway when one of the doctors walked in.

"Are you John Warren's mother?" he asked.

"I'm his guardian. How is he?" she asked brushing the tears from her cheeks.

"He's going to be okay. He has a broken arm and a few scratches, but he's going to be just fine. He's a very lucky little boy."

Lily turned to me and wrapped her arms around my waist. She rested her forehead against my chest and whispered, "Thank God. I thought I lost him."

"Can we see him?" I asked the doctor.

"Yes, I'll show you back to his room. I want to keep him under observation, so we'll keep him here overnight."

"Thank you, Doc," I told him as we followed him down the hall. I looked back to my brothers and hoped that we'd hear something about Courtney soon. "Let me know if you hear anything," I called back. Several of them replied that they would, and I prayed that it would be good news. I really liked Courtney, and I would hate for Bobby to lose her.

A nurse was holding JW when we walked into his room. As soon as he saw Lily, he reached out his arms for her. He had a little blue cast on his left arm, and a few monitors were attached to his chest. Lily ran over to him and took him into her arms. She started kissing his little head and whispered "I'm so sorry" over and over.

"Your son is a tough little guy," the nurse told Lily. "He's been such a trooper through everything."

"Thank you for taking such good care of him. I was out of my mind with worry," Lily explained.

"You'll need to take him to an orthopedic doctor in a

few weeks to have the cast removed. Otherwise, he's just fine. I'll give you some time alone with him. Just buzz the nurses' station if you need anything."

"Okay. Thank you," I told her. I walked over to them and gave JW a kiss on his forehead. "You had us worried, Little Man." He laid his head on Lily's shoulder, and his eyes started to close. He was exhausted.

"He's okay," Lily said looking over to me.

"Yeah, he's okay. Why don't you lay down with him for a little while? He's wiped."

"I thought I lost him," she said with tears streaming down her face.

I lifted my hand to her face and told her, "But you didn't. He's fine." She nodded, and I said, "Now, lay down and get some rest. You both could use it."

"What about Courtney? Do you think she'll be okay?" she asked.

"I'm sure she'll be fine. They'll call me when they hear something. Now, get some *rest*."

Lily and JW had been sleeping for about an hour when I received my first text from Bishop.

Bishop: Out of surgery. Taking her to ICU.

Me: Okay. Keep us posted.

JW woke up the next morning having a screaming fit. He did not like that damn cast, and he was bound and determined to get it off. Lily tried to calm him down, but nothing she was doing was working, so I walked over and lifted him out of her arms. I released the monitor from his chest and started walking him down the hall.

He quickly became interested in all the people walking around and totally forgot about his cast. I stopped by the nurses' station to let them know what was going on. Lily was following close behind, so I decided to go by the waiting room to check on the guys.

Bishop and Tessa were sitting with Bobby, and I could tell he hadn't gotten any sleep. The man looked like shit. "How's she doing?" I asked.

"They won't let me see her," Bobby said frantically. "Why won't they let me see her?"

Bishop looked up to me and shook his head. Damn. It'd been over eight hours. I didn't have a good feeling about it.

"I'm sorry, man. Surely they'll let you back there soon. We're praying for her," I told him. Lily walked over to him and wrapped her arms around his neck hugging him tightly. He didn't even move. He was lost in his own thoughts, and it was hard to watch.

A police officer walked into the waiting room and headed straight for Bishop. Bishop nodded his head and followed him out into the hall. I decided to follow them in case Bishop needed me.

"It wasn't a deer," the police officer told him.

"So what was it?" Bishop asked.

"There were no deer tracks, but we did find several motorcycle tracks. It looks like someone ran her off the road. It wasn't an accident."

"What the fuck?" I said.

"Has your club had any threats lately?" the officer asked.

I knew Bishop wouldn't say anything about the Black Diamonds. He looked over to me, and I already knew what he was thinking. Those guys would be dealt with, and soon.

"Nope. Not sure what's going on, but I'll find out," Bishop said firmly.

"If you do hear something, let us know." He shook Bishop's hand and left.

"Let's keep this between you and me for now. Crack Nut doesn't need to worry about this shit right now," Bishop told me.

"Agreed." I had a bad feeling. We both returned to the waiting room. Bobby never even looked up. It was time to get JW back to his room. The nurses were going to wonder where we went.

"Lily, we need to get JW something to eat. Bishop, let us know if anything changes."

As soon as we started down the hall, Lily asked, "What was that all about?"

"The wreck wasn't an accident. I'll tell you more about it later," I told her as I followed her back to JW's room. I accidently walked right into her when she stopped frozen in the doorway. I could hear the fear in her voice when she said, "No! You can't be here!"

I held JW firmly against my chest as I nudged her to the side and made my way into the room. Maverick was sitting on the small hospital bed shaking his head from side to side. I was surprised by the lack of anger in his face. He didn't look like a man that was ready for a fight. Instead, he looked like someone who had just had their world turned upside down.

"Someone needs to tell me what the hell is going on," Maverick told her.

CHAPTER 21

LILY

"SOMEONE NEEDS TO start talking," Maverick said sounding frustrated.

"What are you doing here?" I asked.

"I got a call from this hospital saying that *my son* was being treated here. They said my name was on his birth records. My *son*? What the hell are they talking about?" he asked.

"You didn't know?" Goliath asked him.

"I have no idea what the hell they're talking about. Is that him? Is that really my son?" he asked.

"What do you mean you didn't know? You threw Hailey out on the streets as soon as you found out she was pregnant!" I shouted.

"Never knew. I honestly never knew," he said looking devastated. "I loved her. I really did, but she was so messed up, Lily. She was always fucked up on something. When she started stealing from the club, she didn't leave me any choice. I had to break it off with her."

"She was on the drugs because of you! You got her hooked on them!" I told him. I was getting angrier by the minute, but there was something about him. I didn't want to believe him, but I knew he was telling the truth.

"Lily, you have to hear him out," Goliath told me. I could tell he believed him, too.

"I don't have to do a damn thing! She needed him, and he was too much of an asshole to help her."

"I didn't know. I would've tried to make it work. Get her some help. Something. I wouldn't leave my kid like that," he explained.

"We're going to need some time to sort through all this. We've all had a long night, and JW needs to get some rest," Goliath told Maverick.

"I can't believe I have a son." A sad look crossed his face as he got up and walked over to Goliath. I couldn't get over how much he looked like JW. There was no question that he was the father. I'd never seen green eyes like that. Maverick stared at JW for a moment and said, "He looks so much like her." He looked down to the ground and shook his head in disbelief. He wrote his number down and handed it to Goliath. "I'll give you some time, but I'm not leaving town without my boy."

No, I wouldn't let that happen. I wouldn't let him take JW from me. There had to be some way out of it. I took a deep breath and tried to think rationally. If Maverick was telling the truth, then he had every right to take John Warren. I knew that, but I didn't know how to convince myself to let him go. I shouldn't have wanted to keep him from his father, but deep down, I didn't care. I couldn't lose him. I wouldn't let him go.

"Lily?' Goliath asked pulling me from my thoughts.

"He can't have him, Goliath," I said firmly. "I don't care what he says! He's not taking him from me!"

"We need to hear him out," he said calmly.

"No, we do *not*! I'm not letting him take John Warren away from me."

"Hear me out," Goliath said as he took my hand and led me over to the small sofa. After laying John Warren down in his crib, he came back and sat down next to me. He took my hand in his and said, "I had Bobby look into him a few days ago."

"And?" I asked.

"There's nothing. He's never been in any trouble, and his club is a lot like ours. I think your sister may have been lying about him."

"Why didn't you tell me?" I asked.

"I wasn't sure about anything yet. I told Bobby to keep looking. I was hoping that he would find something that would prove your sister was right about him. There just isn't anything."

"So, all that stuff he said was true?" I asked.

"There's no way we'll ever know the whole story, but I think he's telling the truth, Lily." Everything Hailey had ever told me was a lie. She had been so strung out, she didn't care who she hurt. I felt my chest tighten at the thought of losing JW. I had grown to love him like he was my own. I couldn't imagine him being taken from me.

"What am I going to do?" I asked.

"I'll do what I can to buy us some time, and I'll see what else I can find out about him. Once we have all the facts, we'll go from there."

It was hard to even take a breath. I couldn't believe it was happening. "I don't know if I can do this. I love him, Goliath. He's all I have left of Hailey," I told him curling up into his arms. I wanted him to take it all away, to stop the inevitable, but I knew he couldn't make that happen.

"I love him too, Lil'. We'll figure this out," Goliath said holding me close while I cried in his arms.

Goliath's phone beeped several times, but he didn't move. His arms stayed wrapped around me, his warmth and strength helping me hold on. Finally I said, "You better answer that. It might be about Courtney."

He looked down at his phone and said, "I need to get down there."

"What's going on? Is she okay?" I didn't think my heart could take much more.

"It's not good. She isn't waking up. She's in a coma. I need to go down and check on Bobby. I'll be back as quick as I can." He gave me a quick kiss on the lips and headed down the hall. I got up from the sofa and walked over to JW. He was sleeping soundly, totally unaware of the chaos going on around him. I lightly ran my fingers over his sweet head and tried to fight back the tears. I needed to be strong for him. Whatever happened, I would always be there for him. Always.

CHAPTER 22

GOLIATH

WHEN I WALKED in, Bobby was pacing back and forth across the waiting room floor. His fists were clenched at his sides, and it looked like he was just about to lose it. I knew he was hurting, so I decided to leave him be. He had to come to terms with this on his own. I walked over to Bishop and took a seat beside him.

"He's having a hard time," Bishop said tilting his head over in Bobby's direction.

"Why won't they let him see her?" I asked.

"He told them he was her fiancé, but they aren't letting anyone back while she's in the ICU. Hopefully they will move her to a regular room soon."

"Good. I don't think he's going to be able to wait much longer," I said. Bishop shook his head. We both knew that Bobby was pretty level headed, but he had his breaking point. We all did.

"Maverick showed up today," I said looking over to Bishop.

"What the fuck? What happened?" Bishop asked.

"The hospital called him. His name was listed on

JW's birth records. He must have flown here last night. He was waiting for us when we got back to the room earlier," I explained.

"He cause trouble?"

After I told him everything Maverick had said, Bishop replied, "You believe him?"

"Yeah, I do. Bobby never found anything on him, so he's got a clean record. I'm going to keep looking just to be sure."

"Call Lily's dad," Bishop ordered.

"You think he knows something?" I asked.

"If not, he should be able to find out. His club is in the same town. He's bound to know something."

"Thanks. I'll give him a call," I said as I stood up to leave. "Lily's having a hard time with this. The guy said he isn't leaving here without his son, and I can't say that I blame him."

"Let me know how things turn out." I nodded and headed back upstairs to Lily. She was feeding JW, and she seemed to be putting on her best poker face as she smiled and talked to him. I was proud of her for pulling it together for the little guy.

"How's Courtney?" Lily asked as I walked over to her. I put my hand under her chin lifting her lips up to meet mine.

I gave her a brief kiss before I answered, "Still no change. She's in the ICU, and they aren't letting anyone back there to see her. Bobby's a wreck."

"Bless his heart. I know this has to be hard on him," she said lifting the spoonful of baby food up to JW's mouth. He scrunched his nose and spit it right back out. That green slime looked pretty damn gross. Hell, I didn't blame him for spitting it out.

"He doesn't like that shit. You got anything else you can feed him?" I asked.

"You know he only likes applesauce and peaches. He has to eat his vegetables sometime," Lily said.

"Give him what he likes."

"Goliath…."

"Seriously babe, give him what he wants. He can eat his vegetables another day," I told her. I knew she was right, but I wanted him to be happy. My stomach twisted into knots when I thought about Maverick being the one to feed him. I didn't want that to happen any more than Lily did, but it was a real possibility. While he was still with us, he should have whatever he wanted.

"Okay," Lily said as she tossed the jar of green peas in the trash.

She was searching in her bag for another jar of food when I said, "You need to call your dad."

She looked up at me and questioned, "Why?"

"See what he knows about Maverick and Hailey. He lives in the same town with them. Maybe he knows something."

CHAPTER 23

LILY

D AD PICKED UP on the first ring, "Hey, honey. How ya doing?" he asked cheerfully.

"I've been better," I told him.

"What's going on?" he asked.

"Maverick showed up here today. It's a long story, but he's here, and he wants JW," I said, my voice trembling.

"I'm sorry to hear that, sweetheart. I know you've gotten attached to the little guy."

"I'm so confused. I just don't know what to think. Do you know anything about this guy? He said that everything Hailey told us was a lie," I asked.

"I was afraid of that," he told me. I could hear the disappointment in his voice as he said, "Lily, your sister was in some trouble. She came here asking for money the week before she died."

"Why would she come to you for money? She could have asked me," I told him.

"She was pretty strung out, and she was trying to buy more drugs, Lily. It was pretty bad. You gotta know she was desperate if she had to ask me for money."

"That can't be right. She was checking into rehab! She was getting help!" I tried to explain, beginning to wonder if I knew my sister at all. Each new thing I found out was opening another hole in my heart.

"Lily, she was just like any other person that's addicted to drugs. She'd say anything to get her next fix. She lied to everyone. She did a real number on Maverick and his club. She's lucky they didn't retaliate."

"I can't believe I fell for all of her lies. I believed in her. She was so convincing. Mom fell for them, too."

"Lily, she was your sister. What else were you supposed to do?"

"I was supposed to know she was lying, Dad. I feel like such an idiot…."

"You can't do that to yourself. She wasn't the sister you knew and loved."

"What about Maverick? Do you know anything about him?" I asked.

"He's a pretty decent guy, Lily. Our clubs have done some business before. Just trying to live by the brotherhood and do what they can to get by. They aren't perfect by any means. Hell, none of us are," Dad explained.

"What should I do? He said he wants JW."

"Lily, you have to go with your gut on this one. Maverick is his father. I think he deserves a chance to get to know his son, one way or another." That wasn't what I wanted to hear, but I knew he was right.

"This is just too hard. I don't want to let him go, but I know it's not right to keep him. If I let Maverick take him, will you keep an eye on him? Make sure JW's okay?"

"You know I will. You can always come here and see for yourself, Lily. I'd love to have you here to get to know the woman you've become."

"Thanks. I might just take you up on that."

"Lily... I'm proud of you," Dad said, his voice gruff. The tears instantly filled my eyes. I never realized how much I needed to hear those words, and it meant the world to me that he finally said them.

"Thank you, Daddy. Talk to you soon," I told him as I hung up the phone. I felt Goliath's arms wrap around my waist as he hugged me from behind. He didn't have to say a word. Just having him close to me, helped me realize that I wasn't alone and that eased some of the hurt. Everything I'd ever thought about my sister was a lie. She lied about everything – to me, to Mom. Damn. I needed to call Mom. I knew it didn't make sense, but I was having a hard time not blaming her for some of it. As Hailey's mother, she should've known something wasn't right. Then, maybe we could've helped her. I hated even thinking about it. It was like losing Hailey all over again.

"We need to call Maverick. We need to figure this shit out," Goliath said.

"I know. I can't believe this is really happening. How am I supposed to let him go?" I asked.

"Legally, he has every right to be with his son, Lily. We have to hear him out. Let's see what he's got to say," Goliath replied.

"Do you think he will still let me see him? I won't be able to survive this if he tries to keep him from us."

"I'm sure he won't have a problem with us seeing him. I'll make sure of it. I'm going to check with the doctor to see when they are going to release JW, and then I'll call him."

"Thank you. I couldn't do this without you," I told him.

He kissed me on the forehead and said, "You have me. We're in this together, Lily. You're it for me." I watched him walk out of the room. My mind kept replaying his words. There was so much going on in my head. I was terrified at the idea of losing John Warren forever. I just prayed that Maverick would let Goliath and I continue to be a part of his life. Because all I really understood at that moment was that I was completely and totally in love with the giant of a man walking away from me.

Goliath arranged for Maverick to meet us at the house at 7. I ran down to check on Courtney one last time before we left. They'd moved her to a new room, so Bobby was finally able to see her. Tessa was right by his side, hovering over Courtney. I knew she was worried about her friend. I hated to see her worried like this, but the doctors told everyone that she was stable. They weren't sure why she was still in the coma, but her vitals were good and they were hopeful. The guys worked out a plan to take turns coming back to the hospital to check on her. It was nice to see that these men really did take care of their own.

Maverick knocked on the door at exactly 7 o'clock. Goliath got up and opened the door letting him inside. "Can I grab you a beer?" Goliath asked before he sat down.

"That'd be great," Maverick replied. He seemed a little nervous which surprised me. He was about to change our lives forever, but he was the one that was nervous?

Goliath returned from the kitchen with three beers in his hand. I took mine and turned to Maverick. "Before we start, I just want to say, I love John Warren. When I left with him, I truly thought I was protecting him. I made a mistake in trusting Hailey."

"You should have told me about him," Maverick said with anger in his voice.

"Under the circumstances, I'd think you'd understand why she did what she did." Goliath said firmly.

"It would have saved us all a lot of trouble if she'd just come to me first. She should've given me a chance, but I understand why she did it. I know how persuasive Hailey can be."

"You're right, Maverick. I should've given you a chance, but I truly thought I was doing the right thing. I loved Hailey, and I never thought she could do something like this. It breaks my heart that she's done this to all of us. I really wish I would have done things differently," I tried to explain.

"I was with Hailey for over two years. For a long time, she meant everything to me. I wanted to spend every minute I could with her. I even thought that I wanted to marry her, start a family with her. First she started taking pain meds for her migraines, then she started smoking pot. Over time, she just kept needing something stronger. In the end, she would risk anything for her next hit. Eventually, she chose drugs over me. Over my son."

"I'm so sorry. I really am," I told him. I knew it must've been hard on him, too. He obviously loved her, and she'd hurt him, time and time again.

"I'm not saying I'll be the perfect father, but I'll do whatever it takes to make him happy. *No matter what.*"

"Do you have people around that will help you? You know, taking care of a baby isn't easy," I tried to explain.

"I do, and I'm very aware that this won't be easy." Maverick replied.

"When exactly are you planning to head back home?" Goliath asked.

"My flight leaves first thing in the morning. I plan to take him back with me then."

I felt the pressure building in my chest, and it was making it hard for me to breathe. It was really happening. He was taking him. I was losing him, and there wasn't anything I could do to stop it.

"He stays here tonight," Goliath demanded.

"I can live with that, but I'll be by first thing in the morning to pick him up," Maverick said as he stood to leave. He walked over to the sofa and knelt down on one knee in front of me. "I know this is hard for you. I can't imagine how difficult it's going to be for you to let him go, but this is something I gotta do. He's my son. I have to try to do right by him." He slowly stood and leaned over kissing my lightly on my temple. Tears were streaming down my face as I watched as he walked out the front door.

I wanted to hate him. I wanted to think of him as some kind of monster for taking John Warren away from me, but the truth is, I really liked him. I can see why Hailey fell for him, but it didn't make it any easier. I got up and headed to John Warren's room. He was asleep in his crib, his little broken arm resting above his head. He's so precious when he's sleeping. I wanted to commit every detail of his little face to my memory—his long eyelashes, little round cheeks, his little fingers, and the beautiful eyes. I lifted his tiny hand up to my mouth and placed a small kiss in the palm of his hand. I brushed the back of my fingers against his cheek loving the feel of his soft skin. My heart ached. I could feel it shattering to a million pieces as I watched him sleep.

Goliath's warmth surrounded me as he walked up behind me wrapping his arms around my waist. He lightly kissed my shoulder and whispered, "Are you okay?"

"No," I said turning around to face him. I rested my head in the center of his chest and began to cry. I was so tired of crying, but the tears just kept coming. Goliath leaned down and slipped his hands under my knees lifting me up into his arms. He carefully carried me to my room and laid me gently on the bed. He walked out without saying a word and headed across the hall only to return with John Warren still sleeping in his arms. He laid him in the middle of the bed before walking over to the other side of bed and lying down. We both turned facing John Warren.

He ran his fingers through my hair and whispered, "I'm sorry, Lily," He sounded completely defeated. I knew he was having a hard time too. It was in his nature to fix things, but he couldn't fix this. Fate had intervened, and there was nothing either us could do about it.

"This is going to be so hard. How am I supposed to just let him go?" I asked.

"You'll do it because it's the right thing to do. Maverick seems like a good guy. I think he'll do right by JW. It's going to be hard, but we'll go see him whenever you want," he said reassuring me.

"Promise?" I asked.

"Promise."

CHAPTER 24

GOLIATH

IT DIDN'T TAKE long for Lily to drift off to sleep. She'd spent most of the day and night crying, and it'd taken its toll on her. I laid there staring at them both. It was hard to imagine what it would be like waking up there without JW in the house. I'd gotten pretty attached to him over the past few weeks, and it was going to be hard to see him go. I gave him a kiss on the head and carefully got out of the bed.

I went into his room and started packing his things. I knew it would be hard for Lily to sort through them, so I figured it might make it a little easier on her. I got everything loaded into JW's bags and put them by the front door. I went into the kitchen and filled his diaper bag with the remaining baby food jars and formula. I wanted to make sure Maverick had everything he needed on their way back to Washington.

When I had everything packed, I crawled back into bed with them and tried to get some sleep.

With everything rolling around in my head, I didn't figure I'd get much sleep, but I woke up to JW trying to crawl across my chest. He was smiling and obviously happy to find me laying there beside him.

"Hey, Little Man. You ready to get up?" I whispered.

Lily opened her eyes and panic spread across her face. "What time is it?" she asked.

"It's about 6:30. He should be here soon."

"I need to get his things ready! We need to change him and get him some breakfast!" she said frantically.

She was about to get out of bed, when I reached over and grabbed her arm. "You stay here with him. I already packed up all of his things and got the diaper bag together for Maverick. I'll get his clothes and get his breakfast ready," I told her.

"When did you do all that?" she asked.

"Last night," I told her as I leaned over and kissed her on the forehead. "I'll be right back."

"Goliath...."

"Today is going to be hard for both of us, but we'll get through this together, Lily."

I grabbed a diaper and a change of clothes and took them over to Lily before I headed into the kitchen. By the time I had his food out on the table, Lily walked into the kitchen carrying JW on her hip. As soon as she fed him, Maverick knocked on the front door. A darkness instantly filled the room. Without saying a word, she got up and let him in bringing him into the kitchen.

Maverick walked over to JW and lifted him up out of the high chair. "You ready to go big guy?" he asked him.

"We packed a few things for him. Everything you need should be in the bags by the front door," I told him.

"Thanks man. I appreciate that. Gonna need to get going. I'll keep in touch. Lily…." He walked over to her and said, "I want you to know that you both can come see him anytime you like. I want you to be a part of his life."

"Thank you for that, Maverick. I'll try to come see him after Christmas if that's okay?" Lily said weakly.

"Love to have you both anytime," Maverick said as he started walking towards the front door. He was about to open the door when Lily cried, "Wait!" She rushed over to Maverick and took JW from his arms. She hugged him close to her chest and gave him several kisses as she said, "I love you so much! I promise I'll come see you soon. Promise." She finally released her hold on him and gave him back to Maverick. "Please take good care of him."

"I'll do my best," Maverick said.

It was excruciating watching him load JW's belongings into the back of that cab. I wanted to stop him, to tell him to fuck off, but as much as I hated to admit it, I knew he deserved to be with his son. When the cab pulled off, Lily ran to her room and shut the door. I could hear her muffled cries, and a part of me wondered if she needed this time alone. I couldn't stand to leave her like this, so I opened the door and walked over to the bed. She was curled up on her side crying. I laid down on the bed beside her and pulled her over to me. I held her as she cried herself to sleep. I knew there was no way I could sleep right, so I carefully slipped out of the bed being careful not to wake her.

After a few hours, she came out of her room and asked, "Can we go see Courtney? I need to get out of this house for a little while." Her eyes were red and swollen from crying, but she'd fixed her hair and makeup. She was trying.

"I think that's a good idea."

It was getting too cold for my bike, so we had to take Lily's car to the hospital. I really hated her damn car. It was too fucking small, but I didn't have a choice. At least it was a short drive to the hospital. When we walked into the waiting room, Renegade and Taylor were sitting with Bulldog.

"Hey man. How did it go this morning?" Renegade asked.

"It was tough, but we got through it. It's gonna be hard not having him around." I'd called Bishop to let him know what was going on. Apparently he had shared the news with the guys. It was nice to know that my brothers were there for me when I needed them. I nodded down the hall towards Courtney's room and asked, "How's she doing?"

"No change. She's stable, but still in a coma. They are calling in a specialist in the morning. They want to run some tests," Renegade explained.

"How's Bobby doing?" Lily asked.

"Dude's having a rough go of it. Never seen him like this before," Renegade answered.

"He's really crazy about her," Taylor said. "There's no doubt about that now."

Taylor motioned over to Lily and said, "Come sit. Tell me all about Maverick."

Lily sat down and said, "He looks so much like John Warren, and he really seems to want to do right by John Warren. I actually kind of liked him. He even said I could come visit any time I wanted."

"That's so good, Lily. You'll have to do that," Taylor told her.

"I will. My dad lives in the same town, and he said I could stay with him whenever I wanted. It's just going to be hard not seeing him every day, you know? I feel like a piece of me is gone. I'll miss him so much."

"I know, honey, but at least you still get to see him. It'll all work out," Taylor said trying to reassure her.

"I hope so."

We stayed at the hospital for a few hours, and I told Renegade that we'd be back tomorrow. It was time to get Lily home.

CHAPTER 25

LILY

A S SOON AS we walked through the front door, I took Goliath's hand and led him back to the bedroom. I needed him. I needed him to take this shitty day away. I stopped when I reached the bed and began unbuttoning his shirt.

He looked at me with concern in his eyes and asked, "You sure about this?"

"I want you to make love to me, Goliath. Long and slow. I want you to help me forget," I pleaded removing his shirt from his shoulders. It dropped to the floor, and I began working on the buttons of his jeans. He watched as I slowly lowered them to the floor. I carefully eased his boxers down below his waist and gave him a gentle push letting him know that I wanted him on the bed. He sat down and watched as I pulled my shirt over my head and threw it to the side. I untied the drawstring of my sweatpants and let them fall to the ground pooling at my feet.

I slowly lowered myself between his legs, and took his cock in my hand. I stroked it up and down before I gently brushed my tongue down the length of his long shaft. A deep hiss filled the room as I took him in my mouth. I continued to move my hand along his length as I fucked him with my mouth. I continued nipping and sucking every inch of him as his moans filled the room. His hands fisted in the back of my hair as he guided me, showing me the rhythm that he wanted. My knees trembled with excitement when I felt the muscles in his legs tighten, and I knew he was about to cum. I was ready to take all of him when in one swift motion, I was lifted up and thrown onto the bed. Goliath hovered over me and said, "As much as I like having your mouth, I'd rather be buried inside of you when I cum."

I felt his breath against my chest and I braced myself, waiting for him to take what he wanted – but he didn't. He was taking his time. He slowly began kissing every inch of my body, licking and sucking, taking his time to torture me with his mouth. I was losing my sense of control when he finally settled himself between my legs. He deliberately brushed his cock back and forth over my clit, teasing me until I couldn't take it anymore.

"Please, Goliath!" I shouted.

That was all it took. With one quick, hard thrust, he was buried deep inside me. His moves were slow but forceful as he eased himself in and out of me. I liked that he was trying to give me what I asked for, but I needed more. I was wrong when I told him I needed it long and slow. I really needed him to fuck me – hard. Make me lose all control. I dug my nails into his ass, urging him to move faster. A deep moan vibrated through my chest as his hands reached up into my hair demanding my mouth. His rhythm increased, but it wasn't enough. "Harder!" I cried.

He put his hands under my ass lifting me up so he could drive deeper inside, giving me all he had to give. My body clenched around him as my climax finally took hold. He continued to pound against my flesh taking me completely over the edge. I cried out his name as he finally found his own release and collapsed on top of me. Our bodies were dripping with sweat, limp from exertion. I trembled under him, reeling from the intense orgasm he had just given me. He lifted himself up on his elbows and said, "You're gonna be the death of me."

"But what a way to go, right?" I said laughing.

"Abso-fucking-lutely," he said rolling to his side. He pulled me over to him, and I rested my head on his shoulder.

He lifted himself up on his elbow and stared at me for a moment. He brushed the back of his hand down my cheek before he leaned down to kiss me. His mouth pressed against mine with such intensity I thought I would burst into flames. I could kiss him for hours. I loved the feel of his lips against mine. His tongue brushed against my bottom lip one last time before he said, "I love you, Lily. More than I ever thought possible."

"I love you, too. So very much. You just keep getting better."

"I'd do anything for you, Lily. Anything."

CHAPTER 26

GOLIATH

T HE NEXT FEW days, Lily did everything she could to keep herself busy. She started working overtime at the bar, and when she wasn't working, she was at the hospital spending time with Courtney. All the distractions were helping, but I knew she was hurting. It was obvious from her swollen eyes that she'd spent her afternoons crying. She didn't like to talk about it, and just the mention of JW's name seemed to set her off. She was missing him. Hell, I was missing him. I could only hope that things would get easier soon.

Bishop wanted us to meet again for church, so he could tell the guys about Courtney. We all decided it was time to figure this out. Sheppard and Bulldog were going to go scope out the Black Diamond's warehouse and see what they could find out. We needed to figure that shit out before anyone else got hurt.

Christmas was in a few days, and I wanted to plan something special for her. I called Lily's father to make plans for us to go for a visit after the holidays. I figured it would help for Lily to have something to look forward to. He said that he'd been by to see Maverick. There was something in his voice that bothered me, but he did his best to convince me that JW was doing fine. He was pretty pleased to finally meet his grandson, but there was definitely something he wasn't telling me. I didn't waste any time picking up the phone to call Maverick.

"Hey man, how's it going?" Maverick asked.

"I was just about to ask you the same thing," I told him.

"I'm not gonna lie. It hasn't been easy, but we're adjusting. It's always something, you know?" Maverick said. He wasn't giving me much to go on, and that concerned me. I decided not to push. I'd find out for myself soon enough.

"I want to bring Lily up for a visit. Give her something to look forward to. Maybe after the holidays."

"Yeah, I could make that work. I know JW would love to see her," Maverick said, his voice sounded strained.

"We'll see you in a few days, but Maverick… call me if something comes up. I'll do anything for JW."

"I know that, man. See you soon," Maverick said as he hung up the phone.

I decided to go by to see Crack Nut on my way back home. I wanted to see how he was doing, but with everything that's been going on, I hadn't really had a chance to talk to him. He was sitting by the bed holding Courtney's hand when I walked into the room.

"How's she doing?" I asked.

"Better I guess. Hard to tell when she won't wake up

and tell me how she's doing," he said. He obviously wasn't sleeping, he looked exhausted.

"You making it okay?" I asked.

"Nope."

"Bobby, she's going be okay. She just needs time to heal. You just gotta be patient," I told him. I really hoped that she'd pull out of this. I don't think Bobby will ever get over it if she doesn't.

"Goliath... I've been such a goddamn idiot. I took her for granted. I should've told her. She should've known," he whispered.

"What are you talking about, man?" I asked.

"I was going to make it official, make her mine. I had her jacket and everything, but I just kept fucking waiting. You know... wanting the perfect time... the perfect day... that perfect moment. I just didn't want to fuck it up."

"Bobby, you'll still have your chance. Don't be so hard on yourself. She knew how you felt."

"I don't know what I'll do if she doesn't come out of this. I won't be able to live with myself," he said tears pooling in his eyes.

"There's no way to know what's going to happen here, but my gut tells me, Courtney is going to be fine. I'm sure she'll be talking your ear off in a few days, and everything will be back to normal."

"You really think so?" he asked.

"I do."

"Thanks man. I really hope you're right."

"Why don't you go home and get a shower. I'll sit

with her for a while."

"I'm good. Not ready to leave just yet, but I appreciate the offer. You get back to Lily. I heard about JW. That's gotta be a tough one."

"It is, but we're dealing. You let me know if you need anything."

"You know I will. Tell Lily I'll be thinking about her."

"Will do," I told him as I headed out the door. It amazed me how one accident had changed all of our lives so much.

I told Lily that I needed to go by and check on my mother. It was Christmas Eve, and I hated the thought of her being all alone. She could tell that I wasn't looking forward to going over there. She wanted to go with me, but I told her it wasn't a good idea. I had no idea what state she would be in, especially around the holidays.

I was surprised to see that all the lights were on, and there was even a Christmas wreath on the front door. Not what I expected at all. I didn't bother knocking. As I walked in, I was shocked at how clean the place looked. I glanced over and saw Mom sound asleep in the recliner. I was about to go check on her, when Bryce suddenly entered the room.

"Hey, Bro! Where you been?" Bryce asked.

"What the hell are you doing here?"

"Gonna be staying here a while. Jennifer kicked me out a few days ago," Bryce said nonchalantly.

"What do you mean she kicked you out? Why?"

"Beats the hell outta me. I finally made partner at the

firm, and the bitch kicked me out. Nothing ever made her happy," he said sarcastically.

"Uh, yeah…I figure there's more to it than that," I scoffed, glaring at him.

"She was always complaining I was never home enough, but she sure as hell liked the money that I was bringing home."

"Well, sometimes money isn't everything."

"Yeah, this coming from someone who doesn't have any," he snorted mockingly.

"Fuck you, Bryce! You don't know shit about me. I'm not going to sit here and argue with you. Just came to check on Mom. Enjoy your visit, shithead."

"Okay, okay. Jesus, I was just fucking around. I'm doing the best I can. I'm finally trying to help out here. Ha… even got Mom to eat something today. I'm trying, man…I'm trying," he finished remorsefully.

I sighed loudly before I shook my head and said, "Alright, man, I got it. Being here with her isn't gonna be easy. You've gotta really look after her. Give me a shout if you need me. I gotta get back." I turned to leave before he could say anything else. I wasn't in the mood to hear his sob story. I appreciated his effort, but he'd been too far up his own ass for too long. He hadn't earned my trust or respect yet. He'd have to do a whole lot more than cooking dinner to get that.

After I left Mom's, I swung by and picked up Lily. We picked up a few last minute gifts and grabbed dinner. Bishop had mentioned that the guys were planning to have their annual Christmas get together tonight. They'd considered canceling it since Courtney was still in the hospital, but Bobby encouraged them to go ahead with the party. He wanted his brothers to celebrate the holiday, even if he couldn't be there with them.

"Are you sure you wanna go home?" I asked. "They're having a Christmas party at the club, tonight. Doc's running the bar, so you can just enjoy yourself for a change."

"That sounds like fun, but… I'd really rather just go home," she said quietly. "I just want to lay down for a little while. I've been feeling a little sick to my stomach since lunch. I think I ate too much."

"You barely ate anything, Lily," I told her.

"I've been feeling a little… off for the past few days. I'm sure it's nothing."

"I knew you were doing too much. You need to take it easy for the next few days."

"I will. I don't have to work until Tuesday, so I have plenty of time to rest. Can we just go home and watch a movie or something?" she said smiling.

"I think we can manage that."

I made her a spot on the sofa and let her pick out some chick flick for us to watch. She laid her head down on the pillow and rested her feet in my lap. She was focused on the movie, but I just couldn't get into it. I kept thinking about her present under the tree. I thought opening it might cheer her up, so I reached under the tree grabbing the small envelope. I laid it on her lap and said, "Open it."

"What… I can't! We have to wait until tomorrow!"

"Open it, Lily."

"Are you sure? You know this is breaking all Christmas traditions," she said. I nodded my head and she quickly started opening the gift. She slowly peeked in the envelope and a look of surprise crossed her face when she realized there were plane tickets inside.

"What is this?" she asked.

"Tickets to Washington. We're going to see JW next week. I made arrangements with your dad, and Maverick is expecting us."

She jumped up and threw her arms around my neck and shouted, "This is perfect! I love it! Thank you so much!"

"We'll leave on Tuesday. I already told Bishop that you'd be gone for a few days, and he said he'd take care of it."

"You never stop amazing me, Goliath. This is the nicest thing anyone has ever done for me. Thank you so much."

"It's for me too, you know. I want to see him just as much as you do."

She rested her head on my shoulder and whispered in my ear, "I love you, Goliath... for so many reasons."

I kissed her forehead and said, "I love you, too, baby. Now, lay back down and let's finish this movie. I want you all rested up before I take you to bed."

CHAPTER 27

LILY

—◦◦◦—

THE OVERPOWERING SMELL of bacon filled the entire house, and it instantly made me feel sick to my stomach. I barely made it to the bathroom before I got sick. What the hell? I opened the medicine cabinet and pulled out the thermometer so I could check my temperature. I heard Goliath cooking in the kitchen as I waited for the beep. The thermometer said I didn't have any fever, so I wasn't sure what was going on. I stood there trying to think what could be wrong with me... when it finally hit me.

Panic rushed through me as I tried to think back to when I had my last period. I just couldn't remember. So much had happened over the past few weeks that the dates were swimming in my head and I couldn't remember. I ran into the bedroom and searched for my birth control pills. I opened the package and was relieved to see that all of the little white pills were gone. I didn't miss any of them, so I should start my cycle any day now. I was just about to toss the container in the trash, when I looked down and noticed the date. My heart started to race, and I felt weak in the knees when I realized the refill date was six days ago. I sat down on the bed and started berating myself for being so stupid. I must have forgotten to take them while I was traveling. I needed to get a pregnancy test as soon as possible.

"Lily?" Goliath called.

"Be right there!" I shouted as I jumped up from the bed and grabbed my bathrobe. I decided not to mention anything to Goliath until I took a pregnancy test. Hopefully, there wouldn't be anything to worry about. Maybe it was just a stomach bug, and life would go on as usual.

I walked into the kitchen, and he had a huge breakfast waiting for me. Damn. It was sweet of him to go to all the trouble, but it made my stomach twist in knots. There was no way I was going to be able to eat.

"You hungry?" he asked with a bright smile. How was I supposed to tell him no?

"Mmm… I could eat a little," I told him.

"You're still not feeling well?" he asked.

I didn't want to worry him, so I said, "I'm fine. Just still trying to wake up."

"How 'bout some coffee?"

"That sounds perfect." I walked over to him and took the coffee mug from his hand. I kissed him lightly on the lips and sat down at the table. I looked down at the table, and those damn yellow, slimy eggs made my throat feel tight. I felt the saliva building in my mouth as I watched Goliath load his plate with tons of bacon and eggs. I swallowed hard trying to muster up the strength to get through breakfast without getting sick. I'm sure I had turned three shades of green by the time Goliath reached for the sausage gravy. I lost it when he started to pour that white clumpy goo all over his biscuit. I shot up from my seat and ran back into the bathroom.

I knew Goliath would start asking questions. There was no way he was going to just let this go. He was standing outside the door waiting for me, and I needed to think of something I could say to stall him. I slowly eased the door open, and just like I thought, Goliath was standing at the door waiting for me.

"You feel up to going into town?" he asked.

"Yes, I guess so, …but, why?" I asked.

"Just go get ready."

"Goliath, it's Chris…."

"It won't take long," he replied before I had a chance to protest.

I really just wanted to crawl back into bed, but I knew how he was when he had his mind set on something. I changed clothes, put on my coat, and headed to the car. I had no idea where he planned to take me this early on Christmas morning, but he was determined to go. He was already in the driveway waiting for me when I stepped outside.

"You going to tell me where we're going?" I asked.

"Nope," he answered flatly. I was beginning to think he was pissed at me. I didn't know what to say to him, so I just got in the car and waited to see where he was taking me. He pulled up to the only convenient store that was open in town. He opened his door, and nodded his head telling me to follow him inside. When we reached the front door, he reached for my hand and led me into the store. He took me straight to the pharmacy section and stopped.

He looked over all the shelves, and then turned to me and asked, "Which one should we get?"

I looked on the shelf where he was staring and felt like the village idiot when I finally realized he was talking about the pregnancy tests. I guess I didn't do a very good job trying to hide all this from him.

"I have no idea. Let's just get one of each," I told him as I picked up the three different tests.

"Good plan," he replied following me up to the cash register. I'd never been so nervous about anything before in my life.

We rushed back to the car and headed back home. The tension in the car was almost more than I could stand. Goliath still wasn't talking, and I had no idea what he was thinking. It could turn out to be really bad. I wanted our first Christmas together to be special, but now I had no idea how things were going to turn out.

Goliath followed me to the bedroom and watched as I opened the three pregnancy tests. I carefully read the directions, and without saying a word, I headed for the bathroom. When he started to follow me, I held up my hand to stop him. "No way," I said. "You are *not* going in here with me. I'll bring them back out when I'm finished."

He grunted, but still didn't say a word. His silence was so frustrating. I said a thousand prayers as I walked into the bathroom alone. Truthfully, I didn't know what I wanted to happen. A part of me would really like to have a baby with Goliath. He was wonderful with John Warren. I had no doubt that he would be a great father, but the logical side of me knew it was way too soon for us to have a baby together. I know that I love him, but we were really just getting to know each other.

When I finished taking the tests, I walked out and laid them on the dresser. Goliath's eyes were glued to those damn tests. He stood there frozen, staring at them lost in his thoughts. I couldn't stand it.

"Look... I can't stand here waiting like this. Let's go into the living room. I want to give you your Christmas presents."

By the look on his face, I knew he didn't like the idea, but he agreed. I raced into the living room and grabbed his first gift from under the tree.

As soon as he sat down on the sofa, I handed him his first present. "Here ya go. It isn't much, but I thought you'd like it."

A small smile spread across his face as he opened the small box. He pulled out the leather band and began inspecting it. It was a dark brown leather cuff that I had engraved with the Devil Chaser's insignia. I thought it was pretty cool, and I knew it would look great on him.

"This is awesome, Lily. I love it," he said snapping it onto his wrist.

"It looks great! Wait... I have two more," I said reaching under the tree. "Now, this one is supposed to be kinda funny."

He gave me a questioning look as he opened the box set of Will Ferrell movies. His laughter filled the room as he looked through each DVD.

"You did good, babe. Really good."

He was still looking through his new movies when I handed him his last gift. I knew they weren't much, especially compared to what he had given me, but I loved seeing him happy like this. He quickly tore into the wrapping paper opening his last gift. He pulled out the Harley Davidson winter gloves and slipped them on. He looked them over, and said, "I think I like these the best."

"I'm so glad you like them," I said as I leaned over to kiss him on the cheek. He wrapped his arm around my waist pulling me into his lap. He put his mouth close to my ear and whispered, "Possibly the best gift you could give me is waiting for me in that bedroom. I've waited all I can stand to wait, Lil'."

"You mean you aren't mad?" I asked.

"Mad? Are you fucking kidding me? You having my kid is best gift you could ever give me," he said lifting me up off the sofa. He grabbed my hand and pulled me down the hall.

I couldn't believe it. He really wanted this. He actually *wanted* to have a baby with me. The closer we got to that bedroom door, the more I really hoped that I was pregnant. I wanted to have Goliath's baby.

CHAPTER 28

GOLIATH

MY HEART WAS beating faster with every step I took. I knew the timing was all wrong, but I didn't fucking care. I wanted it. My eyes were fixed on Lily as she slowly walked into the room, and I could barely stand it as I waited for her to check the tests. A slow smile spread across her face as she lifted them up to check the results.

"Goliath?" Lily asked.

"Tell me…" I warned. She'd kept me waiting long enough.

"They are all…" she smiled trying to stall, but when I stepped towards her she shouted, "*positive!*"

It took a second for me to comprehend what she was telling me. Positive…Fuck. I was going to be a father. It was finally happening. I was going to have the family I'd always dreamed about. I reached over to Lily and pulled her close to me.

"Best Christmas ever," I whispered in her ear.

"You sure you're okay about all this?" Lily asked.

"Absolutely," I told her with no reservations whatsoever. "What about you?" I asked.

"Absolutely," she said as she pressed her lips against mine. I'd always loved the way she kissed, but today was different. Today, she was carrying my child, and that made it all so much better.

"I love you, Goliath."

I placed my hand on her flat tummy imagining what it would look like in a few months, and I said, "I love you, too, Lil'." I wanted to take her to bed and celebrate the good news, but we didn't have time. We were supposed to be over at Bishop's in less than 30 minutes.

"We gotta get going. Bishop will be pissed if we're late," I warned.

"Shit! I forgot all about going over there. Give me twenty minutes," she shouted as she ran towards the bathroom. Once she shut the door, she yelled, "Hey Goliath?"

"Yeah?"

"You're gonna be a daddy." I shook my head in disbelief. Me? *I* was going to be a father. Yeah, this was the best Christmas ever. Damn, I didn't care if we were going to be late. I had to have her. *Now.* I dropped my clothes to the floor and walked into the bathroom. Steam from Lily's shower was already filling the room when I opened the door to the shower. Lily released a small gasp when she turned and saw me standing there. God she looked good standing there with water dripping off her tits. A sexy smile crossed her lips as I stepped into the shower and made my way over to her. I lifted her up, pulling her legs around me, and rested her back against the tile. I didn't think I would ever get enough of that woman. I spent the next hour trying, but I left that shower knowing I'd need her again later that night.

We were late to Bishop's, but it was absolutely worth it. We made it just in time for lunch. Lily's morning sickness had finally calmed down enough for her to actually eat something. She'd need to make a doctor's appointment next week to make sure everything was okay, but I'd heard that morning sickness was actually a good sign.

After lunch, everyone gathered in the living room to open presents. Whenever someone opened a gift, Lily would look over to me and smile. We both knew that we were already given the best gift of all. The only thing that could make the day any better would be JW. If Little Man were there, it would've been the absolute perfect day.

Lily was talking to Tessa about the trip the next week, so I decided I would go over and check on Crack Nut. I turned to Bishop and said, "I'm gonna head over to the hospital for a while. You need anything while I'm out?"

"Tell Crack Nut we're meeting for church tonight at 7. As much as I hate to meet on Christmas, we need to get this shit sorted. Tell him about the accident. It's time that he knew."

I nodded my head and looked over to Lily. "Keep an eye on her while I'm gone," I told him.

"You got some news you'd like to share?" Bishop asked. Damn. Never could keep anything from the guy.

Creeped me the fuck out.

"Not yet," I told him and headed for the door. I wanted to keep this gift to myself – even if it was for just one day.

Bobby was looking a little better. He even looked like he'd had a shower.

"Hey man. Y'all having a good day today?" I asked.

"Pretty much the same. Her fingers are twitching a little more today. I'm really hoping that's a good sign," Bobby said as he took her hand in his.

"I need to talk to you about something," I started. Bobby looked up at me and waited for me to continue. "It's about Courtney's wreck… It wasn't exactly an accident."

"What the fuck are you talking about Goliath?" Bobby shouted.

"The police went by to investigate the wreck. They came by the other day and said there were no deer tracks. It looked like she was run over the road… on purpose."

"Why are you just now telling me this?" Bobby snapped as he stood up from his chair.

"It was a bad time. Didn't think you needed to…."

"That's not your call!" he shouted. He was pissed, and I didn't really blame him. I'd wanted to tell him earlier, but Bishop thought it was better to wait.

"Look, you're pissed. I get that, but you're gonna have to rein that shit in. We need to figure out who did this. We're meeting for church tonight at 7. Bishop wants you to be there."

"Whoever did this is going to pay," Bobby said.

"They're gonna wish they never came near her."

I patted him on the shoulder and said, "We'll make sure of it. Be at the club at 7."

He nodded, and I turned to leave. I looked back over to him and said, "Praying for her, brother. I really hope she pulls out of this." Courtney's parents were walking down the hall as I was heading towards the parking lot. It had to suck spending Christmas in a fucking hospital. Hopefully, she would wake up soon, and it would all be over.

Lily looked exhausted by the time I made it back to Bishop's. It was time for me to get her home. I only had an hour before we were supposed to meet at the clubhouse. We thanked Bishop for having us over, and I told him about the conversation with Crack Nut. He wasn't surprised. Hopefully we would get a plan together tonight, and figure out how we were going to deal with this new club. They were a problem that needed to be eliminated.

"Time to head home, Lily," I called out to her. She stood up and gave Tessa and her kids a hug before walking over to me. I took her hand and led her out to the car. On the way home, she rested her head on my shoulder.

"You need to get some rest, baby. You look tired," I told her.

"You really need to work on your compliments, Goliath. I don't know if I can take much more of your flattery," Lily said laughing.

"You know I think you're beautiful. No one compares to you, but it's obvious that you are spent. Besides, I need to run to the clubhouse for a little while."

"Okay," she whispered.

"I won't be long. We'll try out one of those Will Ferrell movies when I get back."

"I'd like that."

I followed her inside and made sure she was settled before I headed over to the club. I wasn't looking forward to leaving her, but we had to get this shit settled. Crack Nut was going to want revenge for Courtney, but we didn't need to do anything we'd regret later.

CHAPTER 29

LILY

I WAS SO tired I could barely keep my eyes open and it was only 6:30. I grabbed my favorite blanket and laid down on the sofa. My mind went straight to Goliath. I was worried about him. When he'd left, I could tell he had something weighing on his mind. I knew he was worried about the club, but he hadn't talked to me about it. I wished that I had asked him about it, but I doubted he would've told me. He didn't have to tell me that his brothers meant the world to him. I already knew that he'd do anything for that club. They felt the same way about him.

I turned the TV on looking for my favorite Christmas movies. When I saw the kid in the bunny suit, it reminded me of spending Christmas at home with Hailey and Mom. Damn! I couldn't believe I'd forgotten to call Mom. She had no idea about JW. I reached for my purse and grabbed my cell phone. It rang several times before her voicemail picked up.

"Mom, it's Lily. You need to call me. It's about John Warren…. It's important." I hung up the phone and curled back up in my spot. I thought back to my time at Tessa's house. She had a wonderful family, and I loved spending time with her kids. She was so excited when she talked about taking the kids to the mountains. They were leaving first thing in the morning, and they planned to stay there for the rest of her Christmas break. She found a little chapel in Sevierville, and they were getting married while they were there. I loved seeing her so excited about marrying Bishop. He'd made her a very happy lady, and I loved him for that.

Without thinking I started rubbing my hand across my belly. It wouldn't be long before Goliath and I had our own little family. I couldn't believe how much my life had changed in just a few short months. I was truly happy. In fact, I couldn't imagine anything in this world that could've made me happier than I was right at that moment.

I closed my eyes hoping that I might be able to fall asleep, but my stomach kept growling. I rolled over to my other side, but it just wouldn't stop. I gave up trying to sleep and tossed my covers to the side heading for the kitchen. For the first time in days, I was actually really hungry, so I made a peanut butter and jelly sandwich and grabbed a few bags of chips. With my arms filled with junk food, I went back to my spot on the sofa. My favorite Christmas movie was still on, so I decided to watch it until Goliath got back.

It wasn't even eight o'clock when I heard a car pull into the driveway. I was expecting it to be Goliath, so I was surprised when I heard the knock on the front door.

When I pulled the blinds to the side, I could see that whoever was here left their car running. I took my chances and opened the door. I was stunned when I saw Maverick standing on my front step. His arm was in a sling, and he had cuts and bruises all over his face and hands. I didn't know what to think. My heart started to race when I thought about all the reasons why he would show up like this. Something had to be wrong. Without even saying hello to him, I reached in my pocket for my phone and dialed Goliath's number.

He answered on the first ring, "Lily? You okay?" he asked.

"Can you come home?" I asked.

"What's wrong?" he asked.

"I'm fine, Goliath. Just please come home," I pleaded.

"Be there in five," he said just as I heard the engine start on his motorcycle.

I turned my attention back to my surprise guest and said, "What happened Maverick? Why are you here?"

"I need to talk to you and Goliath. Is he on his way back?"

"He said he'd be here in 5 minutes. Come on in and we'll wait for him inside," I told him.

"Give me a second. John Warren is still sleeping in the car. Let me go get him."

"John Warren? He's here with you? Is he okay?"

He didn't respond as he turned and headed for the car. I watched as he opened the back door, and pulled John Warren out of his car seat. I couldn't wait any longer. I raced over to Maverick and

"He's here. I can't believe he's really here!" I cried.

John Warren looked up at me and smiled. He reached for the collar of my shirt and squealed. I was so excited to see him.

"I don't understand. You have to tell me what's going on, Maverick?" I asked.

"Let's go inside and wait for Goliath."

Maverick reached into the backseat and grabbed John Warren's bags throwing the straps over his good arm. I was beyond confused, but I did my best to hold back my questions until Goliath got here. I followed him through the front door and watched him set John Warren's bags on the floor. We were just sitting down on the sofa when I heard Goliath's bike pull into the driveway. I got up and met him at the front door.

"Goliath…." I said stopping him at the front door. His eyes searched over John Warren looking for any signs that something was wrong. He finally looked over to Maverick noticing his arm and bruises.

"Maverick, what the hell is going on?" Goliath asked.

CHAPTER 30

GOLIATH

CRACK NUT WAS completely losing it over Courtney's accident. He was hungry for revenge, and most of us agreed with him. We just needed to make sure we had all had a level head so no one else got hurt. He didn't see it that way. He spent the afternoon finding out everything he could about the Black Diamonds. There was more to this new club than we realized.

They were based out of Detroit, and they weren't exactly a club. The Black Diamonds were a gang, and they had every intention of expanding their territory with any means necessary. They liked to move into small towns and used fear to gain control of the area. These guys were young and stupid. I knew we could use that to our advantage, but it would take time. Crack Nut didn't like that. He was hell bent on making his move now, and he wasn't backing down. Renegade was trying to talk some sense into him when my phone rang.

I left without saying a word to anyone. I didn't like leaving when things were so heated between my brothers, but I didn't have a choice. The tone in Lily's voice concerned me, and I wasn't going to waste any time getting to her. As soon as I got on my bike, I texted Bishop. I wanted him to be ready in case I needed him. I had no idea what was waiting for me at Lily's.

I got a sick feeling in my gut when I didn't recognize the car in the driveway. I parked my bike and headed inside. When I walked through the front door, I was not expecting to see Maverick sitting there. I'd just talked to him a few days ago about our visit, and he didn't mention anything about coming here.

"Maverick, what the hell is going on?" I asked. He looked like shit. His arm was in a sling, and bruises covered his face.

"I need to talk to you. Both of you," Maverick said. "I really don't know where to start."

"Start with what happened to you," Lily said as she walked over to the sofa and sat beside him. "Are you okay?"

"Yeah… it's nothing. I trusted the wrong guy, and it cost me," Maverick said looking down towards the floor.

"You gonna tell us why you're here?" I asked.

He shook his head from side, trying to search for the right words to say. After a few seconds of silence, he said. "I can't do it to him," He ran his fingers through his hair and looked truly distraught. He looked over to Lily and said, "I love him, Lily. I really do. I love him enough to know that he needs more than I can give him right now." He stood up and started pacing back and forth, clenching his fists as he thought about what he was saying. "I let Hailey down. I should've done more.

Should've protected her. I fucked up. I don't deserve to have JW. I'll just fuck it up."

"You're being hard on yourself. Hailey made those choices. Not you. No one blames you." Lily told him trying to calm him down.

"I do. I should've been there for her. Instead, she sank into the darkness where no one could save her. I can't let that happen to JW."

"What exactly are you saying?" I asked him.

"I came here to see... to ask if... I wanted to know if you and Lily would take John Warren, raise him as your own. I want to be everything he needs, but I know I'm not. I can't give him what you can."

"But why now?" Lily asked.

"Lots of reasons. More than I care to explain. Let's just a say a baby doesn't exactly fit in the life I'm living right now."

"Are you sure about this Maverick? You have to know that I want him, but I need you to be sure," Lily said.

"He means the world to me. He's the one truly good thing I've done with my life, and I hate the thought of losing him, but I can't do that to him. He deserves more."

"Maverick, we'll want to adopt him if he stays with us. You gonna be okay with that?" I asked. Lily looked over to me with surprise on her face. A small smile spread across her face when she realized what I was saying. Now, she knew I wanted him just as much as she did.

"I get that. Yeah, I'd be okay with that, but I still want to see him. I want him to know who I am, so he will understand why I did this." he said with a concerned look.

"You will always be welcome here, Maverick. I want John Warren to know you. It takes a special kind of person to love someone enough to let them go," Lily said with tears in her eyes.

"I wish I could be more. I wish I could be the father that he needs, but I know you both love him. You'll give him the kind of life he deserves."

"We'll do our best. I can promise you that," I told him.

"Thank you for trusting us with him. We'll do everything we can to make him happy," Lily said. JW reached out his hands for me. I walked over and took him in my arms. He rested his head against my chest like he was meant to be there. I ran my hand over his little head and pulled him closer to me. I couldn't believe we had him back. I kissed him on the head and said, "Glad you're back Little Man. We missed you."

Maverick got a pained expression on his face as he watched me with JW. He cleared his throat and said, "I'm going to head back."

"You can stay here tonight," Lily offered.

"Thanks Lily, but I need to get back. We've got some shit going down back home, and my president needs me to get back. I'll be in touch."

"Okay, but you are more than welcome. The door is always open. Just let us know when you want to come back for a visit."

"I'll be back. You can count on that. If you ever need me, I'm just a phone call away. Thank you both. I know in my gut that this is the right thing to do." He walked over to JW and kissed him on the side of his head. He laid his hand on his back and stared at him for a minute. He leaned over and whispered in his ear, "Don't hate me for this. I wouldn't do it if it wasn't the right thing to do. I love you, big guy." Tears filled his eyes as he walked over to the front door.

I gave JW to Lily and followed Maverick out to his car. I knew this had to be hard for him, so I said, "You made my girl very happy tonight. If you ever need anything, don't hesitate to call."

He nodded and got in his car to leave. I watched as he pulled out of the driveway before I walked back inside. Lily had JW in her lap talking to him. Her smile couldn't be any bigger as he tried to talk back to her.

"Do you think he's going to be okay?" Lily asked.

"No idea. Doubt he would've brought JW here if there wasn't a good reason. I'll talk to your dad. See if he can help him out."

"I'd like that. I don't want anything to happen to him." Lily held JW close against her chest and she ran her hand over his soft brown hair. It was hard to believe that he was truly back.

"Lily?"

She looked up to me with tears pooling in her eyes and asked, "Best Christmas ever?"

"Absolutely," I pulled her close and I kissed her on

her temple and said, "In just a few months, you've given me everything I ever wanted, Lily." I rested my hand on her belly and pressed my lips against hers.

Brushing the tears from her eyes, she said, "You've done the same thing for me, Goliath. I love you more than you will ever know."

I pulled her close not wanting to lose her mouth, but JW had other plans. Lily pulled back when JW started to whine.

"You're gonna have to get over that shit, Little Man. She's mine, too. You're gonna have to learn to share," I told him.

Lily shook her head and laughed. "I'm going to get him ready for bed. When he's asleep, I'll meet you in the bedroom. I have something you might like to *unwrap*," she said as she got up and took him into the kitchen.

She was everything I ever wanted in a woman, and I wasn't going to wait around to make her mine. I wanted it all. I would claim her as my Old Lady as soon as possible, but that wasn't gonna be enough. I wanted to put a ring on her finger before we adopted JW. I wanted her to have my last name before she had my child. Hell, I wanted them all to have my name, so there was no question that they were *all* mine.

Revenge is the act of passion;

Vengeance is an act of justice.

Samuel Johnson

BOBBY

CAN'T EVEN comprehend the words that are coming out of Renegade's mouth. The words are just a blur, and I don't want to hear it. I'm tired of listening to his bullshit. He's trying to get me to calm the fuck down. I don't want to calm the fuck down. I want to go down to that warehouse and rip their fucking throats out for what they did to Courtney. Deep down I know he's right. I have to think about the club and find the right way to handle this, but my gut tells me I don't need to wait too long. These guys aren't your run of the mill motorcycle gang, and they're out to take over our territory by any means necessary.

After finally hearing Bishop out, I finally feel like we have a good plan set in place. It's going to take some time, but we'll get these guys. One way or another, they're gonna pay for what they did, and I'm looking forward to watching them all go down in flames.

I went straight to the hospital after church. I'd been gone working on research most of the day, and I was ready to get back. I didn't like leaving Courtney, but her parents promised that they'd spend the day with her. Thankfully, they were already gone by the time I got there.

I hate seeing her like this. She's normally so full of life with her wild stories and funny off-the-wall comments. I miss her. I want her back. I walk over to her bed and pull a chair close to the side of the bed so I can be next to her. I take her hand and rub my thumb across her fingers. I'm exhausted so I rest my forehead on her leg as I talk to her. I'm not sure if she can hear me, but I can't stand the silence.

"We had church today to talk about what we are going to do to the guys that did this to you. I won't let them get away with this Court. I love you so much, and I just don't know if I can stand this much longer. I need you to come back to me. I need you to keep me from falling over the edge. Please baby, come back to me."

I breathe deep and try to tune out the silence of the room. The room is quiet except for the constant beeps of the monitors. They are driving me insane. I hate all these machines they have her hooked up to. They came in last week to do some brain scan on her, but the doctors still can't tell me why she won't wake up. She had a mild concussion, but nothing severe enough to cause her coma to last this long. Sometimes, I think she's just being stubborn.

"Court, please wake up. You've kept me waiting long enough. I need you, baby," I plead with her. I've said it all before, but she never moves. She just lays there with her eyes closed like she's sleeping. Her face is pale, and she's lost so much weight. I hate it. I can't stand watching her fade away right in front of my eyes. It just fuels my need for revenge every time I look at her. My head is still pressed against her leg when I feel her fingertips brush through my hair. I convince myself it's nothing, just the stress of the day getting to me. When I feel it again, I slowly lift my head to see Courtney trying to open her eyes.

"Court?" I whisper. "Can you say something? Let me know I'm not dreaming here, baby. Say something."